"In case someone **continued, "I can**

"So you believe me?" Mackenzie asked.

"Does it matter? Someone may or may not be trying to harm you, and in the meantime I'm going to make sure they don't succeed. The truth will come out in time."

She said nothing.

Aaron looked at her. "Okay, here's the deal. You do exactly as I say and you don't ask questions. If something happens we're not going to stop in order for me to explain it to you, we're just going to run. That's how you stay safe. Got it?"

Mackenzie nodded.

"Until the threat has passed, you stay where I know you are at all times."

"Fine," she said.

Aaron folded his arms, ignoring the screaming pain in his shoulder. She needed to understand. "Now tell me everything—who wants you dead, how you got in the witness protection program, all of it. I'm not messing around and I need to know it all if I'm going to have a chance of keeping you alive."

Books by Lisa Phillips

Love Inspired Suspense

Double Agent
Star Witness

LISA PHILLIPS

A British expat who grew up an hour outside of London, Lisa attended Calvary Chapel Bible College. There she met her husband, who's from California, but nobody's perfect. It wasn't until her Bible College graduation that she figured out she was a writer (someone told her). Since then she's taken the apprentice and journeyman writing courses with the Christian Writers Guild, and discovered a penchant for high-stakes stories of mayhem and disaster where you can find made-for-each-other love that always ends in happily ever after.

Lisa can be found in Idaho wearing either flip-flops or cowgirl boots, depending on the season. She leads worship with her husband at their local church. Together they have two children, a sparkly Little Princess and a Mini Daddy, and two bunny rabbits.

You can Tweet at Lisa (@lisaphillipsbks), or to find out more visit www.authorlisaphillips.com.

STAR WITNESS

LISA PHILLIPS

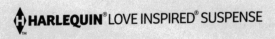

HARLEQUIN® LOVE INSPIRED® SUSPENSE

If you purchased this book without a cover you should be aware that this book is stolen property. It was reported as "unsold and destroyed" to the publisher, and neither the author nor the publisher has received any payment for this "stripped book."

Recycling programs for this product may not exist in your area.

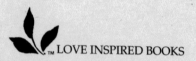 LOVE INSPIRED BOOKS

ISBN-13: 978-0-373-44622-3

STAR WITNESS

Copyright © 2014 by Lisa Phillips

All rights reserved. Except for use in any review, the reproduction or utilization of this work in whole or in part in any form by any electronic, mechanical or other means, now known or hereinafter invented, including xerography, photocopying and recording, or in any information storage or retrieval system, is forbidden without the written permission of the editorial office, Love Inspired Books, 233 Broadway, New York, NY 10279 U.S.A.

This is a work of fiction. Names, characters, places and incidents are either the product of the author's imagination or are used fictitiously, and any resemblance to actual persons, living or dead, business establishments, events or locales is entirely coincidental.

This edition published by arrangement with Love Inspired Books.

® and TM are trademarks of Love Inspired Books, used under license. Trademarks indicated with ® are registered in the United States Patent and Trademark Office, the Canadian Intellectual Property Office and in other countries.

www.Harlequin.com

Printed in U.S.A.

And he came and preached peace to you
who were far off and peace to those who were near.
—*Ephesians* 2:17

This book was written during NaNoWriMo,
and massively rewritten later.
Huge thanks goes to Heather Woodhaven,
who talked me off the ledge many times.

ONE

Mackenzie Winters didn't need her years in witness protection to know someone was targeting her. She was looking at the evidence.

All four tires on her old, nondescript car had been slashed.

Mackenzie glanced up at the dark sky. After the day she'd had, all she wanted was to go home and crash. But that wasn't going to happen anytime soon.

She looked back at the dark building, the center that she managed for at-risk teens. Locked up for the night, it looked almost menacing, but that was crazy. It was only bricks and mortar.

The broken streetlight at the far end of the parking lot cast long shadows on the pitted cement. Mackenzie gripped the strap of her purse and strode around the building to the street, where there was a pay phone that seemed to have been long forgotten.

Downtown Phoenix was busy even at this time of night, and there wasn't much time before the last bus of the day. Mackenzie dropped some coins in the slot and dialed her WITSEC handler's number. Eric would know what should be done about her slashed tires. He'd do what he called a "threat assessment" to determine if she needed to be *really* worried—as opposed to just regular worried.

All because of one night: the night Mackenzie had walked into the hotel suite her entourage shared and saw a man holding a gun to her manager's head. Seconds later, he'd pulled the trigger, and Mackenzie, her manager and her head of security, who'd been with her that night, were all on the floor bleeding. She was the only one who'd survived—the one who had testified against the shooter and crippled a drug cartel in the process.

The call to her handler went to voice mail, so Mackenzie left a message and started walking again.

She scanned the street in front and behind her. The hairs on the back of her neck stood on end. Whoever had slashed her tires could be watching right now, waiting for the right moment to strike. Why else would they make sure her car was undrivable, instead of just slashing one tire and making her change it? They must want her out of her normal routine. But for what?

Paranoia came with the territory, even though it had been sixteen years since the day she'd testified against the shooter. The adrenaline never really left. Not when at any moment you could be recognized, gunned down...or kidnapped and left for dead in the middle of the desert.

Okay, so she needed to watch a romantic comedy tonight instead of a movie about vengeful mobsters.

A car slowed beside where she was walking on the sidewalk, but she didn't look. Traffic was backed up, so it could be nothing. Mackenzie walked faster. It was better to be safe than dead. She should call her WITSEC handler again as soon as she got home. It had been years since she'd needed protection, and months since she'd even talked to Eric on the phone, but if there was a threat, then he should know.

She flicked her gaze to the street. The car was still there, tracking with her every step.

This was her life. It had been ever since her manager had made a deal with the wrong people. It wasn't enough that he'd spent all the money she made him as a musician on his habit; no, he'd needed more money to sustain that habit. And when he'd neglected to pay the money back, the cartel had come looking for him.

Hello, witness protection.

Now for the past two weeks she'd had a funny feeling—nothing more than that, not until the tires. It could be simple vandalism, nothing more. Maybe someone with a grudge against the arts center she'd founded. Since she was still alive, she didn't think it was about her former life. If Carosa found her, he would simply kill her.

Mackenzie knew what it felt like to be watched, and to have her whole life dissected for everyone to read about in the tabloids. But no one would even recognize her now. Mackenzie's WITSEC persona was more of a spinster librarian than a famous musician. To her surprise, she'd found being unassuming felt more natural than all the makeup and sparkly clothes in the world.

The car slowed to a crawl and a window whirred down. Mackenzie's foot hit a crack in the sidewalk. She stumbled and broke into a run. There was only one more block to the restaurant where she sometimes got dinner before she went home. The car engine revved to catch up.

A door opened ahead, and a man stepped out, blowing across the top of his white paper cup. It was Eric, her handler. Mackenzie tried to stop, but she slammed into him. Eric's coffee went flying. She grabbed his arms to steady herself and his eyes flashed wide.

"Someone's after me."

The rapport of gunfire shot toward them like fireworks. The window of the coffee shop shattered, and concrete chips flew up from the sidewalk, stinging her legs. Mackenzie's head spun. She was being turned; Eric had his arms around her. He hit the concrete first, grunting when she slammed into him. They rolled toward the car parked by the curb. Gunshots flew over their heads and people screamed.

When they reached the spot between the parked car and the curb, out of the line of fire, Eric hauled her up on her hands and knees. "Crawl. Go!"

With him right beside her, they scrambled away. The sidewalk cut through her tights, so she got to her feet. Eric's grip on her elbow held her down, lower than the cars parked on the side of the street.

The gunfire stopped, but he still didn't let her straighten fully. Thank God he was here. What would she have done if Eric hadn't walked out of that coffee shop at exactly the right moment? She'd probably be dead, and she owed the U.S. Marshals Service so much already. They'd given her a new life when she desperately needed one. How could she possibly thank him for this?

The engine revved, and the car sped away.

"Okay, I think we're good." His voice was deep, deeper than she remembered, and his proximity warmed her chilled skin. His denim-blue eyes scanned the area and then focused on her. "You can get up now."

He stood first and winced when he touched his left shoulder.

"You're bleeding." Mackenzie gasped. "You've been shot!"

"It isn't from this. I just ripped my stitches is all. Don't worry about it."

"We should call an ambulance."

He checked the street and finally looked at her, his blue eyes almost gray. "What we should do is get off the street."

Mackenzie glanced around. The sound of sirens was getting closer. Probably someone in the coffee shop had called 911. "Do you think whoever shot at me will come back and try again?"

Eric shrugged, as though being shot at was no big deal. "I wouldn't rule it out."

"Are you going to make me leave Phoenix? I like it here."

His forehead crinkled in confusion. It was a nice forehead. What was wrong with her? Eric was her handler; she wasn't supposed to think he was good-looking.

He motioned to the coffee shop. "We should at least go inside."

"Right. People might need help."

Mackenzie needed something to focus on aside from the weirdness that seemed to resonate between her and Eric. That had never happened before.

Eric usually wore a suit and tie. Maybe it was the jeans and a black T-shirt he was wearing that made him different. He seemed relaxed…and tired.

"Is there a reason you're staring at me?"

Mackenzie turned away, praying he didn't see the awkwardness. *So unprofessional.* She spoke over her shoulder as she walked. "I'm going to see if they have a first-aid kit."

Inside the coffee shop, broken glass crunched under her feet. The two baristas and half-dozen customers looked shaken, but no one seemed to be injured.

Eric entered right behind her, probably intent on protecting his charge. He'd always been efficient. It was probably why they gave him the responsibility of working in witness protection.

Mackenzie went to the barista, crouched by an older

man who seemed to be having trouble breathing. "Do you have any medical supplies? My friend is bleeding."

The woman who'd made Aaron's Americano jumped up and ran behind the counter. He stepped away from the crazy lady who'd launched herself at him—that part hadn't been all bad—and tried to ignore the sting in his shoulder.

He crouched in front of the old man clutching at his chest. "Take a breath. Blow it out slow and try to relax."

Outside, the sirens grew to deafening proportions. Aaron turned just as two police cars and an ambulance parked on the street outside. He looked back at the old man again. "Medics are here."

The man's brow flickered. "Army?" His voice was barely audible.

"Yes, sir. Good guess." He wondered what the old man would say if Aaron told him he wasn't just army, but Delta Force. But that wasn't something anyone but close relatives could know.

Aaron glanced around. The crazy lady stared intently at the door the barista had disappeared behind. She looked shell-shocked, which he didn't blame her for, since she'd just been shot at on the street. He'd never seen anything like that stateside, except in the news. It was usually contained to the war zones his team was dropped into, not downtown Phoenix.

Some trip to come and see his brother this was turning out to be. First Aaron's twin was too busy to see him, and then he suddenly had to fly to D.C. for whatever reason a U.S. marshal needed to be somewhere. A federal court case was the obvious guess. Why didn't he know more about what Eric did?

He'd figured they could spend some time together, reconnect. That wasn't going to happen now. Aaron had been bouncing around his hotel room earlier before he ran out for coffee just for the sake of something to do. Anything was better than staring at the ceiling trying to sleep.

EMTs raced in, carrying their bulky bags. Aaron got up and out of the way. He looked at the woman he'd collided with. She dressed kind of dowdy, but she had nice eyes. It was a shame she was loopy, and paranoid. Just because someone had been shooting in her direction didn't mean they were out to get her.

Her arms were folded, the sleeves of her wool cardigan pulled down over her hands. She clutched her elbows, making herself look small. Vulnerable.

Aaron stepped closer to her. "Are you okay?"

She really did look shaken. Maybe all this was for real. He'd have to make sure the cops looked out for her if she really was in some kind of trouble. But what trouble could a harmless-looking woman be in?

Her eyes locked with his. Beyond her, three cops stood huddled on the sidewalk and she motioned to them with a tilt of her head. "What do I tell them?"

"The truth is probably a good plan."

Her face paled. "I guess. Someone did just try to kill me."

She looked as though she believed it. So was she a great actress, or was she really onto something? "The police can help. You can't hold back anything from them."

"Okay. I can do this." She gave him a short nod. "I can tell them I'm in witness protection, if you think it's for the best."

"You're…what?" Aaron sucked in a breath and choked. "Do not tell them that."

A uniformed police officer strode in, all business as though this was an everyday occurrence, and maybe it was. Maybe she hadn't just told him what he thought she had. *Witness protection?* Surely that wasn't something you just blurted out.

Mackenzie's face jerked from the cop to him and her eyes widened, as though she wanted to latch on to him for safety. Why was she looking at him that way?

The cop looked between them. "You folks all right?"

She shifted up on her toes, as though she was anxious to leave. "My name is Mackenzie Winters and someone just tried to kill me."

The cop's eyes widened. "I'm Officer Parkwell. Maybe you should tell me what happened."

Mackenzie. It wasn't the name of a woman you overlooked—it was too special for that. Aaron liked it. She looked at him, as if she was asking for permission. He shook his head.

She should definitely not tell the cop she was in witness protection. Why had she told him? They didn't even know each other. There was probably a procedure to these things. If this Mackenzie woman really was part of that, shouldn't she know what the rules were?

She turned to the cop. "Okay, well, someone tried to kill me. I think they've been stalking me, whoever they are, because they slashed my tires tonight so I couldn't drive home. While I was walking to the bus stop a car pulled up by me, and someone started shooting."

She looked at Aaron and relief washed over her features. "Thank God you were there. I'd be dead if you hadn't acted so quickly."

Aaron shifted his feet. "No problem, ma'am."

It wasn't a big deal. Why was she making it such a big deal? Anyone else would have done the same thing. Just because he'd got them both out of harm's way didn't mean Aaron was someone special.

He knew he wasn't a hero, because heroes didn't ruin

missions and get their teammate hurt. His shoulder injury was inconsequential compared with the fact Franklin wasn't ever going to see again. And it was Aaron's fault.

His first time as leader of their now four-man Delta Force team, and he'd led them right into a trap. The package had been retrieved—eventually—and the information brought home to whoever needed the intelligence, but the success of the mission on paper didn't make the reality any better. Not when Aaron had been shot and Franklin blinded by shrapnel. Sure, they couldn't have known there would be that level of resistance at the plant they'd infiltrated, but they were trained to be prepared for anything.

The truth was that while Aaron had been a spotless Delta Force solider for years, when the responsibility of leading the team was on him, he'd frozen. And the cost of that hesitation, that moment of trying to decide whether to continue on or abort had been high. Too high.

The cop looked up from his little pad at Mackenzie. Her eyes were on the EMTs carrying the old man out on a backboard. "I'm sorry people got hurt. I didn't know." She looked at Aaron, tears in her eyes. "What do I do now?"

"How should I know?" Why did she persist in looking to him for help? Did Mackenzie really think he knew how to help someone in witness protection? He was on vacation, not some kind of hero for hire.

"You're not going to help me? You're just going to abandon me? What if they come for me again, what if they... kill me?"

Aaron motioned to the officer. "That's what the cops are for. They'll be able to keep you safe. I've got a life to get back to." Not to mention a career to rebuild, and a whole lot of reparations to make.

She blinked and a tear fell down her cheek. He didn't want it to prick his heart, but it did. The last thing he needed was a vulnerable woman looking up at him with brown eyes that really were too big for her face.

Aaron cleared his throat and turned to the cop. "You have someone who can look out for her?"

The officer nodded. "Of course. If you'll wait here, I'll inform my sergeant that Ms. Winters feels that this wasn't a random shooting and that her life is in danger."

He walked away and Aaron looked at Mackenzie again. "We'll get you squared away, don't worry about it. No one's going to hurt you."

"You're really not going to help?"

This again? Why did she think it had to be him who kept her safe just because he'd thrown her to the ground while bullets were flying? That was nothing but a reflex.

He couldn't let the hurt on her face get to him. He sighed. "Look, you seem nice and all, but I think you've got the wrong end of the stick here. I'm not your hero."

She swiped away tears that were still falling. "Of course you are, Eric. You're the only one who can help me."

TWO

Mackenzie watched the realization wash over his face.

"You think I'm Eric."

She didn't know what to say. This *was* Eric. Had he hit his head when he pulled her down onto the sidewalk?

"I'm not Eric."

This was bizarre. "Well, if you're not Eric, then who are you?"

The man's lips curled up into a smile, and he stuck out his hand. "Sergeant Aaron Hanning, U.S. Army. I'm Eric's twin brother."

She stared at his hand. What was there to smile about? "I just told you I'm in witness protection."

"How was I supposed to know you were going to say that?"

"I thought you were Eric!"

"That's apparent now, but I didn't know it then."

"This is awful. Eric's going to make me move for sure. I don't want to leave. I like it here. I've lived in Phoenix for years." Mackenzie sucked in a breath to try to get control, but Sergeant Aaron Hanning, U.S. Army, just stood there smiling at her. She put her hands on her hips. "There is nothing funny about any of this."

"You just told me my brother works in WITSEC. I

thought he worked at the courthouse, or ferrying prisoners around and whatnot. This is cool."

"Cool? It's going to get out. I'll be exposed. My life is over because of you."

"Me?" He glanced around the room, and then sighed and looked back at her. "Look, I'll call Eric. We'll get this figured out. Get your name removed from the witness statement or something so you're not in danger."

"You'd better."

"Excuse me?"

"This is your fault. I'm already in danger, I didn't need this."

His eyes widened. "I didn't shoot at you. I saved your life. Maybe you should say thank-you instead of yelling at me because you blew your cover to me."

Mackenzie gasped. "It's not a cover, it's my *life*."

"Okay, okay, calm down already."

"Calm—"

Sergeant Aaron Hanning, U.S. Army, put his hand over her mouth. "I'm going to call Eric, okay? He'll tell us what to do, and we'll get you squared away."

She took a breath and nodded. The frustration bled away a little, leaving a sick feeling its place. His eyes flickered, but he didn't look away. He just kept staring into her eyes until Mackenzie reached up and pulled his hand away from her mouth. "Please call Eric."

He blinked and whatever connection they had dissipated. Aaron pulled out his phone and stepped away. He stuck the phone between his ear and shoulder and pulled open the first-aid kit that was on the counter.

Officer Parkwell strode back in, his mouth set in a thin line. "We have a witness that identified the plates of the car your shooter was driving. It belongs to a local gang member. At this point we think it's highly unlikely this was anything but a random shooting. Unless you can think of a reason someone might want to harm you?"

"It could be about the arts center where I work. In fact, I think it is about the center. Someone slashed my tires before they shot at me."

It wasn't a happy thought to consider that she was the cause of someone being hurt. Or that she had grieved someone enough they felt they needed to retaliate and slash her tires. But tensions often ran high at the center. Especially when a person took into account the tough background each of the kids had.

"The performing arts center down the street?" The cop scribbled on his notepad. "Is that where your car is?"

"Yes, in the center's parking lot, around back."

"We'll get someone over there to check it out."

The cop strode out again.

The shooter had followed her before they fired. Was that to confirm she was their target? Nothing about this felt like coincidence. Even if it wasn't related to her testimony all those years ago, it was still about her.

Aaron came back over. "I got voice mail. Eric's been in D.C. the past couple of days. He could be on a plane coming home."

Mackenzie hoped that was it. Because in the meantime, she was stuck with the injured, sarcastic twin brother of the all-American U.S. marshal who was *supposed* to be the one helping her. Why couldn't Eric be here now?

Mackenzie wrapped her arms around herself. It was like being eighteen again, having her whole life end because she'd been in the wrong place at the wrong time. The sound of gunshots from the car had frozen her. Again. She rubbed a hand on her collar, over the place the bullets had entered. She wanted the comfort of a hug, but she'd already gushed over Aaron enough when she'd thought he was Eric.

He'd acted quickly, saving her life. Another "she'd have been dead, if not for…" to add to the long list already in her WITSEC file. But she had to keep her distance, because not only was he a stranger to her, but he didn't seem like the kind of man who appreciated a woman who couldn't stand on her own two feet.

"Are you okay?"

Mackenzie tried to smile. "Sure, I'm fine." It wasn't as if her whole life might be over or anything. "It's just late and it's been a really long day. I didn't need this drama with you on top of it." She looked at the front window. "I hope that man's going to be okay."

He moved close to her side, and then he said, "Me, too. So, listen, if you're going to be fine, then I'm going to head out—"

She whipped around to look at him.

"I'll talk to Eric, and when the police have what they need, they'll probably let you leave."

She was supposed to just go home? Mackenzie swallowed. "Uh, sure. That's fine, I guess. You need to get to the hospital anyway, right?" There was blood all down his sleeve.

He nodded. "Right."

But he didn't leave. Mackenzie's cheeks burned under his stare, so she lifted her chin and stared right back. "You said you and Eric are twins?"

He nodded.

"Uh…that's nice." Probably identical twins—they looked similar enough that she'd mistaken Aaron for Eric. But now that she looked closely, she could see slight differences in the nose, where Aaron's looked as if it had been broken. Her cheeks heated. "I thought you were leaving."

"So did I." His lips curled up, his eyes on her. "And yet I don't seem to have gone yet."

He might think this was amusing, but Mackenzie did

not. He was nice enough looking—okay, so he was down-right gorgeous—but that didn't mean she wanted him to stare at her. He might get the idea that she actually wanted a relationship.

His phone rang.

Aaron reached for his back pocket and hissed. *Ouch.* His medical leave was only supposed to be two weeks, but given how hard he'd hit the sidewalk and rolled, he guessed the recovery was going to be longer.

He stepped away from Mackenzie. "Hanning." The background noise was a steady rush of people and move-ment.

"You called?" Eric's breathing was labored. Was he in a hurry?

Aaron perched on a circular table in the corner. "So… you work witness protection, huh?"

There was a short pause. A door shut and Eric said, "Who told you that?"

"Met a friend of yours tonight. Mackenzie Winters. She thought I was you, but that was after she and I nearly got shot in a drive-by." Aaron rubbed his eyes with his free hand. It was a shame his coffee had spilled all over the sidewalk.

"I got her voice mail, but it didn't say anything about a shooting. I take it you saved her?"

"A gun went off. After I reached for the weapon I wasn't carrying, I just moved us. It was a reflex, nothing more."

What was it with everyone assuming he was some kind of hero? He still hadn't told Eric he was on medical leave or why he'd instinctively fled from anything army related.

Reconnecting with his brother was long overdue, there was no doubt about that. But the real reason he'd come to Phoenix to see Eric was more about what he was going to face when he returned to work. About the fact his teammates wouldn't even let him see Franklin. They'd expected him to apologize before he left, but how did you say sorry when you'd blinded someone? It just wasn't good enough. "I'm not a hero."

Eric sighed. "I'm boarding another flight right now, I'll be back ASAP. Can you stay with Mackenzie?"

"Why? She's fine. The cops are taking care of her. I didn't think this had anything to do with her being in witness protection. She said something to the cop about the center where she worked."

"The likelihood is that it isn't connected with her being in WITSEC. But I'd still like someone watching out for her until I can get there to assess the situation." Eric sighed. "Please do this, Aaron. I really need your help."

Eric wanted him to stick around with Mackenzie longer, when his last failure had cost someone their sight—and their future? "I'm not your guy for this one. Don't you have resources? Surely there's a plan when things like this happen."

"Of course there is, but that was before I spent two days in D.C. trying to get to the bottom of a potential leak in my office."

"No offense, but I'm on leave with an injury. This doesn't really concern me."

"You saved her. She'll trust you, and she needs someone to keep her safe until I can find out if this is related to her past. And find the traitor in my office."

Aaron blew out a breath. "You think a U.S. marshal is responsible?"

"All I have is supposition right now. We can't rule anyone out until the FBI determines who caused the leak of a number of files. It could have come from inside or outside of the office—at this point we still have no idea. We had the FBI warn the witnesses whose names were leaked, and those with active threats have been moved."

"So why was Mackenzie still in Phoenix?"

"Her file was not one of the ones that were leaked."

"So the shooting is unrelated."

Eric's footsteps stopped. "We still have to keep your involvement in this under wraps. If Mackenzie is being targeted for anything, then she should be kept safe. The leak could be a diversion. I can't go through normal channels because everything is balanced on the edge right now. I can't disrupt anything or the FBI case unravels. If there's a mole, whoever it is will bury themselves so deep we'll never find them."

Aaron got to his feet, his eyes on Mackenzie. He might not be a true hero, but there was no way he was going to leave a woman unprotected if he could help it. "What do you want me to do?"

"You'll help?"

"I'm not going to leave you hanging." Maybe this was the chance he'd wanted to connect with his brother. If the cost was reopening the wound in his shoulder, Aaron would gladly pay it. Eric was all the family he had, and at least his brother didn't think he was a failure like his team did. They wouldn't even let him in Franklin's hospital room. "What do I do with her?"

"Keep an eye on her until I get this whole situation figured out. The FBI thinks it should only take a couple of days to track the source of the virus that copied the files. Have Mackenzie stick to her normal routine, but keep your eye out. The cops will do their own investigation to find out if there's a threat against Mackenzie, and I'll be there tomorrow."

Mackenzie turned. Her eyes widened and her cheeks flushed at whatever was on his face. So she wasn't used to direct attention. And why not? She was a pleasant-looking woman; she just downplayed her looks, unlike pretty much every woman Aaron had ever dated.

He hung up and crossed the room to her. "Eric asked me to keep an eye out for you. In case someone is after you, I can make sure you're safe."

"So you believe me?"

Aaron shrugged his good shoulder. "Does it matter? Someone may or may not be trying to harm you, and in the meantime I'm going to make sure they don't succeed. The truth will come out in time."

"Oh." She glanced around the café.

Aaron took gentle hold of her elbow. She was the protectee now, and he would maintain a professional distance.

"Let's walk to my truck." His shoulder needed looking at, but he'd have to find supplies somewhere. He did have extra gauze and bandages in his hotel room, plus no one would know she was there.

He looked around the parking lot as they walked but didn't spot anything suspicious. Eric wanted her safe, and the best option for that was a hotel he already knew was secure. But that was probably the last thing Mackenzie wanted.

"We can stay at your house."

Her eyes widened. "I don't have a guest room."

"I'll sleep in the truck."

"You can't do that. You're injured."

"I've slept in worse places. Believe me." Aaron got the feeling he was going to have to do a lot of reassuring with this woman.

When she'd settled herself into the passenger seat of his truck, Aaron turned to her. "Okay, here's the deal. You do exactly as I say and you don't ask questions. If something happens, we're not going to stop in order for me to explain it to you, we're just going to run."

THREE

By the next morning, Mackenzie had almost managed to forget that someone tried to kill her the night before. But when Eric walked into the Downtown Performing Arts Center, it all flooded back.

Aaron was around somewhere, supposedly protecting her, although she hadn't seen much of him. She hadn't told him anything the night before, but she had convinced him to stop by the E.R. and get stitched up. Mackenzie had driven back to her house and in the end she'd convinced him to spend the night on the couch instead of in his truck. He'd said it was so he could see her front door, but she'd seen the pain in his eyes. Especially considering he'd refused a prescription for pain pills.

"Who is that?"

Mackenzie turned to Eva, who taught classes at the center while Mackenzie ran the office. They were standing at the entrance to the hallway that led to the classrooms. "An old friend of mine."

"What kind of old friend?" Eva grinned. Mackenzie blinked. She hadn't even thought of Eric in those terms before. She supposed he was handsome enough, though Aaron was the better-looking brother. Both of them could be movie stars. The idea that either one would ever look twice at someone like Mackenzie was laughable. "Thank you, Eva. I needed that."

Eva blinked. "What did I do?"

"You reminded me that life isn't all doom and gloom." Mackenzie wrapped her arm around Eva's shoulders. "And that the best things don't ever change."

"You're welcome. I think." Eva stepped back from their huddle, smiling. "I should get to my next class. The natives will be getting restless."

Mackenzie nodded.

"Are we still on for dinner later?"

"Absolutely." Mackenzie smiled, excited to have been invited. Which was good, since anticipation covered the feeling of being a complete ninny because she was all worked up over one dinner. Eva probably went out with her friends all the time while Mackenzie couldn't remember the last time she got invited to hang with someone. Plus it had the added benefit of taking her mind off the fact that someone had shot at her and she now had a permanent shadow in the form of Sergeant Aaron Hanning, U.S. Army.

Eva was one of their best teachers, able to easily relate to the street kids who populated the center. Her application two months ago, after the previous teacher had suddenly quit, turned out to be a blessing Mackenzie never expected.

Mackenzie studied her WITSEC handler as he approached; his suit was still crisp though it was after lunch. But the look on his face said he was about to apologize for something.

"Hi, Eric."

He nodded. "Mackenzie. How are you?"

She motioned behind her. "Let's go to my office."

He followed her in and sat in one of two chairs in front of the desk. Castoffs from a doctor's office. The whole room was smaller than the closet she used to have before she became a federally protected witness.

The brothers weren't much older than her, she didn't think. Eric wore the air of authority that came with the marshal's star badge with ease, while his predecessor had been a burly guy with a gray goatee and a thing for barbecue ribs.

Eric shifted in his chair. "How are you?"

Mackenzie poured Eric a cup of coffee. "Do you think Carosa still wants to kill me, even after all these years?"

He took the cup from her. "If you weren't in danger anymore, you'd have been released from the witness protection program. Carosa is still out to kill you for testifying against his brother." He took a sip and sighed. "I don't want you to be unaware of the reality of the situation. But I did run a check with immigration this morning, and to the best of our knowledge, he's still in Colombia."

"So he didn't shoot at me." Why wouldn't the nausea in her stomach ease? This wasn't about her past. "It was someone else."

"The police think your slashed tires and the attempt on your life were both the work of a local gang. Maybe someone with a grudge against the work the center does with teens, getting them off the streets." He gave her a small smile. "Apparently the car belongs to the brother of Hector Sanchez."

Hector was a regular visitor to the center. "So I might be in danger, but not from Carosa."

"Unless your identity is revealed. If anyone discovers who you really are, or your picture gets in the media, you'll be pulled out of Phoenix." Eric sighed. "We don't want to jump the gun, but the Marshals Service is dealing with an internal investigation right now. It doesn't directly relate to your case, but it's why I asked Aaron to keep an eye on you."

Mackenzie squared her shoulders. "I could leave on my own."

"If you do that, I can't protect you. You'll be leaving the cover of WITSEC and effectively opting out of the witness protection program. That's why Aaron is here."

She squeezed the bridge of her nose. Hadn't she atoned enough already for the person she used to be? For years she'd been so careful to adhere to every rule for life and living. It was as though it didn't even matter.

Eric's mouth curled up into a sad smile. "I really am sorry you're caught up in this, Mackenzie. I know it's the last thing you need. But I'm sure the police will resolve it quickly, and Aaron will make sure you're safe in the meantime."

He shouldn't be sorry. She was the one who'd gotten herself in this mess in the first place. It might have been a case of wrong place/wrong time that caused her to witness a double homicide. But she'd only been there because she'd thought being famous was the ultimate life. Now that the man she testified against had been killed in prison, she should have been able to get on with her life.

Would she ever be free?

Mackenzie squeezed her eyes shut. It was as though God wasn't done punishing her for her selfishness. She read her Bible every day, and when she had made up for what she'd done in her former life, then she would allow herself to fully accept what Jesus had done for her.

"You can trust him, Mackenzie. Aaron won't let anything happen to you."

"He's right. I won't."

Aaron filled the doorway. Mackenzie stared at him, trying to figure out what it was that made him so much more compelling than his brother. It couldn't be physical. She chuckled. "You really look a lot alike."

Aaron glanced at Eric, and they both shook their heads. He'd never seen what people meant when they said that. Apart from the blond hair and blue eyes, their similar features, they were completely different. Aaron's nose had been broken more times than he could remember since he first went skydiving on his eighteenth birthday, whereas Eric liked to *read*.

Aaron turned to his brother. "You have the picture of the guy after Mackenzie?"

Eric nodded and handed Aaron a file. Clearly he hadn't liked the idea of showing Aaron a picture of the brother of the man she put in jail, but Aaron didn't want the guy walking up to Mackenzie on the street and pulling a gun before he even recognized the threat. "You know I don't like going in blind. Ever."

Eric shrugged, as though Aaron's discomfort didn't much bother him. "And you know I can't tell you anything. If Mackenzie wants to share, that's up to her. But legally I can't divulge the details of her case. We don't even know for sure the shooting is related. In fact, I'm with the police on this one. I don't think this is anything more than someone with a grudge against the center. Albeit a dangerous grudge."

Mackenzie came around the desk. "So I can tell Aaron about me if I want, but I don't have to and you're not going to?"

Eric nodded. "In this instance, it would be okay for you to tell him. And, honestly, he can better protect you if he knows."

Great. Aaron wanted the details. How was he supposed to protect her when he didn't even know what the threat was? And she wanted to keep her secrets? That had the potential to kill both of them.

Aaron glared at her and then said to Eric, "I need to know."

Only Eric didn't look as if he was going to give it up. He said, "I can't even confirm whether or not the woman in this room is, in fact, in the witness protection program. As far as you know, she's a friend of mine who has a man in her life who wants to do her harm."

"Right." Aaron studied the photo in the file. Middle-aged man, Hispanic, his hair sprinkled with gray. Aaron committed the image to memory the way he'd done with so many photos of targets before, and then passed the file back to Eric.

"You need anything else?"

"Can't think of anything." If Mackenzie wasn't going to tell him, Aaron would have to get the information some other way.

Although he would settle for a shoulder that didn't scream with fire every time he moved it the wrong way.

Eric frowned. "I'm sorry I can't tell you how long this will take. I have to go on as if nothing is wrong until we find the leak, but if we hit the point when you have to go back on base, we'll have to deal with that when it comes."

"I called my C.O. this morning, so he knows that for the time being I'm involved in something." And hadn't that been a fun conversation? His commanding officer was known for his brevity, but at least Aaron now knew that Franklin wasn't doing any better than he'd been before Aaron went on leave.

"My lunch break is almost over." Eric turned to Mackenzie. "Be safe, okay? Listen to Aaron. He knows what he's talking about."

* * *

The door shut. Silence stretched out into a minute as Mackenzie and Aaron stared at each other. He looked as though he was expecting something, but she didn't know what. Or she just didn't want to admit she might know what he wanted her to say.

There was a light knock at the door.

"Kenzie?" Eva stuck her head in and glanced between Mackenzie and Aaron. Her full lips tipped up on one side in a half smile. Mackenzie's friend was probably more than confused about the second of two strange men she'd seen with Mackenzie today. "You okay, girl?"

Blood raced through Mackenzie's veins, and her cheeks warmed. "Sure."

Eva's eyes gleamed. She'd be digging later to find out who Mackenzie's male visitors were. Why couldn't her life be boring? Instead Mackenzie had been dragged into this strange play where she didn't know her lines.

"What's up?"

"We're a teacher short. Chris had to rush out. The day care called, and his son, Tim, is puking everywhere. The kids in the blue room are waiting for their voice lesson. I need you to cover."

"No. I can't do it." Paperwork, yes. Answering phones, yes. Fund-raising, no problem. Sing in front of people again? No way. That could get her killed.

Eva's lips thinned. "There's no one else."

Mackenzie glanced at Aaron, but he was pressing buttons on his phone and hadn't seen Eva's face. She looked back at her friend. Eva was the opposite of everything Mackenzie tried to be—sparkly and loud. But right then Mackenzie's closest friend—which wasn't saying much, since they usually only saw each other at work—wasn't happy, to say the least.

"I can't do it."

"Kenzie, do you think I don't know what you're hiding? Do you think I haven't figured it out?"

"I—" It wasn't possible. Mackenzie had worked too hard for too long for her secret to get out now. "I don't know what you're talking about."

"Girl...I heard you sing."

"What?" Mackenzie sucked in a breath. "When?"

"Do you think I'm stupid?"

"Of course not." How could Eva think that?

The other woman's eyes softened. "About a month ago I left my phone here. It was late when I came back to get it. I heard you, playing piano and singing to yourself."

Mackenzie didn't know what to say. It didn't spell total disaster, but her voice was distinctive. She had assumed she'd be safe just working in the office. After all, she'd set the center up. Wasn't that enough to balance the scales? She'd come to terms with the fact that music couldn't be part of her life anymore, except in secret. Now she wouldn't be able to sing at all, not even when she thought everyone was gone.

Why did that hurt?

Eva's head tipped to the side. "You know, you kind of sound like—"

Please don't say it. "I know."

"They're already in the blue room waiting. Please. There's no one else."

Mackenzie sighed. "There's a ton of work to do in here."

It was an excuse, but she had no interest in being the person she used to be. Not again. And she would do everything she could not to fall back into that trap of selfish, wild living. The only thing those days of youth had done was set her on a collision course with this life of hiding and secrets.

"Kenzie—"

She bit her lip. "Okay. I'll go and oversee things. They can practice, and I'll just make sure it doesn't get out of control."

But there was no way she was going to sing in front of the kids. No way on earth.

Eva beamed as if it was Christmas morning. "Great."

Mackenzie rolled her eyes, but Eva didn't see because she'd already breezed out the door. It was only one class. Surely disaster couldn't happen that fast.

"Hold up a second."

Aaron stopped her with a hand on her arm. Mackenzie looked down at his fingers on the sleeve of her sweater. She could feel his heat through the material and it struck her that she'd never felt anything so warm. His hands were strong, his nails trimmed short, and his little finger was bent as though it'd been broken and not quite set straight.

She looked up at his face. "The kids are waiting."

"We still need to have a conversation. I know what Eric said, but if I'm going to have the best shot at protecting you, then I need to know what happened."

"Fine." Even though Mackenzie had no intention of telling him anything about who she used to be.

He apparently didn't buy it, because he said, "If you don't, I will absolutely walk. I have to know what I'm up against." The hint of a smile gleamed in his eyes. "Who knows, I might surprise you."

"I don't like surprises."

FOUR

Aaron leaned back against the wall, listening to a teen girl singing. There really was no other way to keep an eye on Mackenzie without it looking as if he was doing exactly that. Diligence was the only thing that paid off. Faith in a higher being to solve all his problems was nothing but a childish dream. Not when in one split second everything could go wrong and no matter how hard he tried to fix it, someone still got hurt.

He rubbed a hand down his face, dismissing the memories of heat and sand…and blood.

He loved the spontaneity of being Delta Force, though there was a shelf life to the career. Retreating just didn't sit well with him, but when it was that or put his teammates in danger because he couldn't admit he was slowing down…there wasn't anything to it. When the time came, Aaron would just finish up his days and move on with the confidence he'd done his duty to Uncle Sam.

Aaron was almost to his mid-thirties, so it was past time to start thinking about fallback options. Especially considering the fact his team hated him at this point. When he got back, there wasn't going to be much of a working relationship between them all if they didn't trust Aaron anymore.

They'd banded together around Franklin, which was

the right thing. Aaron didn't fault them for giving their support to their blind teammate. Franklin would need it. But did they have to reject Aaron in the process? Hadn't it just been a mistake? A horrific one, sure, but he was only human. Didn't they know that?

"What do ya say?"

Aaron glanced down the hall where a teen boy in a white T-shirt and saggy jeans crowded a younger girl against the wall.

"I'm not sure." The girl's voice was a nervous murmur. "I don't think—"

The boy's face hardened. "Not the right answer, babe."

Aaron sauntered over. "Hey, what's up, guys?" They both turned to him. The boy's face hardened and the girl's eyes went wide. "Is there a vending machine around here? I'm really craving a soda."

The girl's face washed with relief, even though the boy hadn't stepped back. She pointed down the hall behind Aaron. "In the kitchen. They're a dollar, but if you hit the top three buttons on the left and the bottom right one at the same time, an orange soda will drop out."

The boy looked at her. "Why would you tell him that?"

"He's Ms. Winters's new boyfriend. I saw them together earlier."

The boy looked back at Aaron. "For real? You're Ms. Winters's new boyfriend?"

Aaron nearly rolled his eyes at the third degree from a kid who apparently thought his teenage self was something everyone needed to take note of. Was that what he had looked like at that age? Aaron must have seemed ridiculous. It was a wonder his foster parents hadn't laughed at him.

Aaron looked at the girl, admittedly a little intrigued. "Does Ms. Winters have a lot of boyfriends?"

"I think you're the first."

"How long have you been coming here?"

"Like, four years."

That was interesting. So as far as the kids knew, Mackenzie didn't date. At all. Maybe it wasn't just him who noticed the air of "I'm hiding something" that she wore. Or he only saw it because he knew she was in witness protection.

Aaron lifted his chin to the boy. "You might want to back up a step there, champ. Give the girl some breathing space."

The teen's eyes narrowed and he moved forward. Aaron's body tightened in readiness.

"Is everything okay?" Mackenzie appeared beside Aaron, bringing with her the scent of cotton candy. She looked at the girl. "Megan?"

"Everything's fine, Ms. Winters."

Aaron watched the boy step back and wondered how Mackenzie managed to generate that level of respect just by smiling.

"Class is over, so your sister is waiting for you."

The girl scurried around their huddle and disappeared around the corner into the room where Mackenzie had been teaching. Aaron turned back to see Mackenzie had closed in on the boy. "You take care, Hector."

Hector? This was the kid whose brother had shot at them on the street?

"I don't need advice from you." Hector stepped back, motioning with his fingers.

Aaron moved to shut down whatever the kid was about to do, but Mackenzie stopped him with a hand on his chest. "Let him go. He's dealing with enough."

"Like an older brother who tried to kill you yesterday? I'm surprised he even showed up." Aaron blew out a breath. "You shouldn't let him disrespect you that way."

Mackenzie frowned. "You don't think these kids understand love, or kindness?"

"Trust me, they have one currency and that's respect. Nothing else gets through to them."

"You sound as though you know what you're talking about."

Aaron shrugged. "Same world, different city."

"Maybe you could tell me about it later."

"Why? So you can feel as if you know me?" He shook his head. "I'm not one of those kids."

"I know that. Aaron, I just—"

"Thought we should be friends? Is that what you want? Or do you want me to keep you safe from the guy who wants you dead? Because you can't have it both ways. That's not how this works."

Mackenzie stepped back and her face blanked. "I'll be in my office. Try not to start any more fights, okay? I'm only going to grab my purse."

He followed her, unwilling to mess up the only thing that would keep Eric's respect when he found out Aaron was responsible for the failed mission and his teammate's medical discharge. He watched her switch off her computer and shut out the lights. The other woman who worked there—Eva—met them in the lobby.

"So I'll meet you at the restaurant? Or are you going home to change first?"

Aaron glanced between them. "What's this?"

Mackenzie sighed. "I forgot to mention it. I'm really sorry, Eva."

She thought Aaron wasn't going to let her go?

Eva glanced between them before her attention settled on Mackenzie. "But you have to come out. You promised. It'll be fun, I'm telling you. All-you-can-eat appetizers and we'll splurge on something chocolate for dessert even though we don't need it. Come on, what do you say?"

Mackenzie clearly wanted to go. Did she not want him tagging along and putting a crimp in girl's night out? Well, too bad.

Aaron smiled. "Sounds great. I'm in."

Eva's eyes flickered, but she recovered quickly. "Sure, why not."

Aaron stuck his hand out. "Aaron Hanning, nice to meet you."

She shook his hand. "Eva Partez."

"Mackenzie and I'll meet you there. All right?"

Mackenzie swallowed. "Sure."

He grabbed her elbow and led her out before she could change her mind. Mackenzie locked the front doors as Eva sped off in a black Mustang with the top down. The sun had turned the sky pink and Aaron had to sidestep so he could see Mackenzie's face without the glare.

"All-you-can-eat appetizers?"

Mackenzie sighed. "She's been asking me to hang out with her for weeks and I finally broke down yesterday and agreed. I actually thought it would be fun, but now that Carosa might have sent someone to kill me..."

"Carosa? As in the Colombian drug cartel?"

She hesitated for a minute, and then nodded.

"So that's who the guy in the picture was." He whistled. "You don't mess around, do you? But don't worry. I'll be there to keep you safe, whatever this is. That's why Eric asked me to stay."

"Why would you? I mean, it's kind of clear that you don't really like me. Why would you give up your time to protect someone who basically means nothing more to you than some stranger on the street?"

"What I'm protecting is Eric's witness. It's his career on

the line because of your safety. And I never said I didn't like you."

"Seemed kind of obvious to me."

"Well, I'm—" he swallowed "—sorry for that. In the future, I'll try to be...nicer."

Mackenzie laughed. "That was hard for you to say, wasn't it? Big tough guy like you. It must be rough, having to be pleasant."

Aaron didn't like one bit that she was laughing at him. "Let's just get going, okay?" He grabbed her elbow again and headed down the street toward where he'd parked his truck.

"Why do you do that?"

"What?"

"Haul me around like a sack of potatoes."

He loosened his grip but didn't let go. "Guess I need to be nicer about that, too. I don't usually work with people who are willing to cooperate. I normally have to push a lot harder to get the result I want."

"Then maybe you should just try asking nicely."

"Is it going to be as uncomfortable as apologizing?"

Mackenzie laughed. "Probably."

Okay, when her face brightened like that he didn't much mind that she was teasing him. Maybe it wouldn't be so bad having to be around her for a couple of weeks. He could get used to sparring with Mackenzie Winters.

Aaron opened the passenger door for her, like a gentleman was supposed to. Unfortunately that meant they both got a look at the interior. Last night he hadn't been in any shape to apologize for the state of his truck. He'd just shoved everything into the middle to make a space for her. But now he saw exactly how bad it was. The foot well had a bunch of fast-food wrappers tossed there, and the passenger seat was under his jacket, a duffel bag and two gel packs that weren't frozen anymore.

Aaron tossed the duffel and jacket behind the bench seat and motioned to the seat. "Your chariot, my lady."

"Why, thank you, kind sir."

When he pulled out, he scanned the street while Mackenzie stared at him again.

"So what are we going to tell Eva about you? I mean, you did just show up out of the blue, so we can't pretend you're my new boyfriend. What about my cousin?"

He glanced at her and then back at the road. "Why do we need to have a story?"

"Isn't that what people do in these situations? Develop a cover story. Perhaps you could be my cousin from out of town, recently laid off from your job of hunting down rogue skunks in the Alaskan wilderness."

"Rogue skunks?"

"Or something."

He smiled. "Judging by the contents of the bookshelves in your living room, it doesn't surprise me you have a vivid imagination."

Mackenzie folded her arms. "What's wrong with what I read?"

Aaron waved away her question. "I'm not even going to get started on what's wrong with your taste in books. You really don't want to know."

"Well, what have you read lately?"

She probably thought he didn't know how. He smiled. "Dr. Seuss."

"Like when you were six?"

He nearly laughed. "No, a couple of weeks ago. There was this kid in the hospital who had burned his hands, so he couldn't hold the book. I hung out with him a while before I got discharged. Sweet kid."

"Seriously?"

"What? It was a nice thing to do."

"It was."

He pulled across an intersection, about a mile from the restaurant. "And you're the only one who can help kids?"

"I didn't say that. It's just contrary to what I've seen from you before. You were a little…gruff earlier."

"I apologized then."

"And I accepted. I'm just saying—" Mackenzie froze.

A black van came at the front left corner of the truck. Another van came from the right, boxing them in. The two vehicles moved closer together, tightening the noose. Aaron gripped the wheel, fighting to keep them from bouncing off the side of one van into the other.

The vans screeched to a halt, stopping Aaron's truck with them. The door on one van slid back, and Mackenzie gasped as hooded men in black fatigues with big guns poured out. More appeared behind them, cocooning them in the truck. All the weapons were lifted and pointed at Aaron.

"Let the girl out!"

Aaron gripped the wheel with both hands but didn't move or speak.

"Um…Aaron?"

One of the men in all black moved toward her door.

"Put it in Reverse." Aaron spoke, but his lips barely moved.

"What?"

"They can see both my hands. Reach over and put it in Reverse." He pushed out a breath. "Now."

He moved his foot to the clutch. Mackenzie ground the gearshift, wincing at the sound. Before she was barely done, Aaron's foot hit the gas and they flew backward. She screamed and gripped the dash. The truck spun in an arc, Aaron changed gears again and they sped forward. She looked back. "They're right behind us. They're chasing us."

"I know."

"They didn't shoot, though."

Aaron glanced at her and then took a corner so fast they almost went up on two wheels. "You want to talk about this now? Fine. I'm guessing they don't want you harmed. They don't get paid for delivering damaged goods."

"Carosa wants to kill me himself. I know. He yelled it across the courtroom the day I testified against his brother." She took a deep breath and pushed it out slowly as they raced down the street. "This isn't about Hector's brother now. Maybe someone hired him just like they hired these guys."

"Good thing for us Carosa seems to only know semi-competent thugs."

Every few streets she glanced back until finally she said, "They're not there anymore."

"They must have backed off." He pulled into a gas station and out the other side, cutting off a Buick. "That means they're confident they'll get another shot."

FIVE

Aaron drove for the sake of driving, not worrying about where he was going. He reached over and squeezed Mackenzie's hand. "You okay?"

Mackenzie's fingers were chilled, as though the courage had been drained out of her. He let her hand go, wondering what he was supposed to say now that all of this was officially a whole lot bigger than just someone with a grudge against the center. Carosa had sent men for her.

Aaron pulled up at a stoplight. Mackenzie's big eyes made her look more like a scared girl than a woman who dressed like a grandma librarian—except for the black high-heeled boots that started directly under her knee-length skirt. Her hair was still pulled tight in that ugly bun she'd been wearing all day. It was as if it was some kind of uniform she used to protect her identity. Had she been a recognizable person before? He looked at her again, trying to think if there was someone she resembled.

Eric should have pressed the local P.D. harder. Clearly Mackenzie's name had been leaked somehow, given that it had taken no time at all for hired mercenaries to find her. And for what? Aaron didn't even want to think about what Carosa would have done with her. Or how her current identity had been connected to the person she used to be.

Mackenzie looked out the side window. Her fingers gripped the straps of the backpack that sat between her knees. They were on the run from Carosa, but Aaron had no idea what the deal was. What had happened to her?

Ignorance wasn't bliss—it got you killed.

When the danger was hypothetical, that was fine. He'd had the time to wait for her to share. But now that it was real, he didn't like not knowing the people involved, or the fact Eric couldn't give him all the information about Mackenzie and the guy after her without breaking WIT-SEC rules.

Some favor.

He needed to get Mackenzie someplace safe until Eric called to say it was all clear for her to come home… probably only to be relocated again. Who knew what the fallout from this mess would be? Especially when the Marshals Service realized Mackenzie had disappeared.

He studied her while the light was red, trying to guess who this woman really was and why she was hiding.

"I need to know." He clenched his jaw, willing her to talk to him. "Do you know any of the men who tried to stop us?"

"I've never seen them before."

He sighed. "I'm sorry, I had to ask."

"Now you're in danger, too. Because of me."

And that seemed to concern her a great deal. Why, he had no idea. She didn't know him from any guy on the street, just like she'd said of him. Mackenzie cared way too much about a bunch of kids most people would write off—even him, before he'd seen how they opened up to her.

Aaron squeezed her fingers again. "It makes no difference if I'm in their sights, too—the play is still the same. We stick together." He followed the line of cars that clogged the city's streets. "My shoulder's still heal-

ing. Eric didn't know who else he could trust, and we'd
already met."

"What are you healing from?"

"You don't have to worry about that. I'm perfectly capable of keeping you safe until we meet up with Eric and
get the next move all figured out." He hung a right, one
eye on the traffic behind them, watching for a tail.

"Are you sure you're okay with being involved? I mean,
drop me at the next corner if you want. I won't be responsible for dragging someone else down with me." She glanced
away, out the window. "Not again."

Now, why did she have to go and say that? "I might not
be a hero, but at least I'm not a jerk. I'm in this with you,
and I have no intention of ditching just because things got
hot. The threat is real now."

"I know."

"Mackenzie, you don't have to worry. I'm going to stick
with you until we know you're safe. Either Eric will figure
out what's going on or we'll get you a place to stay. Then
you can go back to your life."

Back to the Downtown Performing Arts Center, a building filled with kids and laughter from the moment school
got out until well after dark. Music had permeated the
whole place today—everything from the most somber clas-
sical piece to the latest radio hit song. What was it about
Mackenzie that she could take a broken-down building
and a bunch of kids everyone had written off and infuse
them with so much life?

Aaron needed to know more about why Carosa was
after her so he could wrap up this favor and get back to
his life. But first he had to lose any possible pursuers, just
in case there was someone behind them he hadn't seen.

"Why now?"

Aaron didn't know if she was talking to him, or if she

had even heard what he said. He took a sharp right down an alley and hit the gas. They came out the far side onto another busy main street, and he flipped a quick U-turn to the sound of multiple beeping horns.

It was as if she didn't even notice.

"Why couldn't this have happened years ago, before I made a life for myself? He shouldn't have been able to find me. This shouldn't be happening."

Aaron's chest got tight. "I get that this is a shock, Mackenzie, but it can't be unprecedented. Can it?"

She finally looked at him. "Being ready for what is a remote possibility is one thing. Thinking you're actually going to have to leave the life you love because a group of soldiers is trying to abduct you is something entirely different. I'm done, I won't ever be safe. He found me this time, he'll find me again."

"So that's it? You're going to give yourself up to die?"

She huffed. "What do you expect me to do? I'm going up against a man who'll kill me without a second thought. What do I do in the face of that? Hit him with a guitar? Sing him to death?"

Aaron made a turn onto a major street lined with stores and restaurants. "As entertaining as that would be, you don't have to worry. It's why I'm here."

"And I get to be the helpless female while the big strong man protects me? Sorry, that doesn't work for me."

He pulled up behind a sky-blue Cadillac at a stoplight. The air conditioning took that moment to stop working, and hot Arizona air filled the cab instead. Great.

He turned to her. "If you're going to fight me all the way, maybe you should get out at the next corner. Or you could trust me and I can teach you how to survive."

"Like how to shoot a gun?" She shuddered. "I don't think so."

"Then you seriously need my help. Eric wouldn't have asked me to stick around if he thought you should just give up and die."

"It's his job to make sure I'm safe."

The light was still red. Aaron studied her profile, folded in and wound tight again. "You don't have to be scared."

"I'm not worried about dying, but I'm also too much of a realist. Survival is pretty much a pipe dream at this point. This guy will never, ever give up."

Something dark flashed in his eyes. "You're not going to let me help you?"

She reached for the door handle. Aaron was blocked in, cars behind and in front of him in his lane and the light hadn't changed.

"I'm not letting anyone else get killed because of me. I'm doing this alone."

Mackenzie slammed the door. Aaron jumped out and called her name, but there were no footsteps that followed her. He wasn't the kind of man who abandoned his truck on the street—even if it was a dump on the inside. It had been torture sitting there chatting as though she was going along with the whole thing while she waited for the right time to make her move.

She couldn't trust anyone; that was the bottom line. And there was no way she would put anyone else in danger. Nothing good could come from spending time in an intense situation with a good-looking man who didn't seem like a bad guy, even if he was occasionally a jerk.

Mackenzie needed to save her energy for staying alive instead of falling back into her old ways. Sparks, smiles, then a brief touch of the hand, a light kiss...it might as well be a whirlpool that sucked her under, or a riptide that took her back to the kind of person she had no intention of becoming again.

Mackenzie started down the sidewalk. Traffic streamed past in both directions. It took her a second to get her bearings, but she headed for a bus stop, watching every vehicle that passed for the vans the mercenaries had been driving. When she finally slumped into a seat on a bus, Mackenzie would be able to close her eyes and let herself relax. Buses were anonymous. People left each other alone for the most part, and she would be able to just stare out the window and not think about what her life had become.

Sometimes she rode the bus all day—through the city, out to the desert, tourist bus trips to the Grand Canyon—wondering what would happen if she never got off. The bus would stop eventually, done for the day. She could disembark and hop another bus...anywhere.

If you leave, I can't protect you.

And yet she had left, which meant WITSEC was going to kick her out of the program for breaking the rules. She was off on her own now, no Eric, no Aaron. Fear churned her stomach, reminding her she hadn't eaten since lunch. There was no way she'd be able to stomach anything now. Her life was over and she was as good as dead. Staying with Aaron only meant prolonging the inevitable.

At least this way he would be safe.

A young mom pushing a toddler in a stroller passed her. Mackenzie returned the woman's smile. That could never be her. She'd done too much to ever be free of the chains of her past. She would be forever bound by the consequences of the girl she'd been.

A new life meant leaving behind everything and everyone she had come to love. She should have kept emotion out of it, done her job and gone home at the end of the day to her empty house. Too bad everything about the center kids made her fall in love the minute she looked in their eyes. They might be rough at the corners and some even hard, but they were so full of life and promise.

Something she didn't have left.

Not since she'd testified against the son of a drug lord in a trial that ended with him getting life without parole for double homicide and attempted murder. Then it had all ended four years later in a prison riot. She should have been free because Pedro Carosa was dead. Problem over, except it wasn't. In the years since then, his older brother, Alonzo, apparently hadn't given up the idea of revenge. It seemed he was just as committed as ever to making Mackenzie pay for tearing his family apart.

And there was no way she was going to let anyone else get caught in her cross fire.

The car engine revved, but she didn't turn. It was happening all over again, and this time there was no Aaron to dive with her out of the line of fire.

The vehicle slowed, but she wasn't about to turn that way and allow whoever it was to get a look at her. Mackenzie sped up her pace, her eyes on the road ahead.

How could she get out of here? A side street? Into a café and out the back entrance? Would a bus come along just in time? Maybe a cab.

But what was the point? Carosa had found her.

The vehicle's brakes squealed as it stopped and the driver's door slammed.

She started running.

SIX

"Mackenzie." He didn't like the look on her face when she spun, eyes wide and stark with fear. "You're exposed out here. We have to get somewhere safe."

Her spine straightened. "I told you, I can't go with you."

"So you walk along the street out here, late at night, where anyone can pick you off and make you just another tragic statistic? The guy after you gets exactly what he wants, and your life is over. Great plan."

She flinched, and he knew he'd hit the mark he was aiming for. "If it sounds as if I'm trying to scare you, that's because I am. We can't give this guy the chance to succeed. You said yourself you want to be free of this." He held out his hand to her. "I'm giving you a shot at living the rest of your life, Mackenzie. I know I'm practically a stranger to you, but you can trust me."

Someone brushed past them on the sidewalk, close enough to jostle her. "Can I? How do I know that?"

Aaron studied her. Something didn't jibe with what she said. She inferred it was an issue of trust, but he didn't see fear in her eyes…he saw pain. What had happened to this woman that made her so hesitant to trust someone that she willfully put her own safety in jeopardy? She pushed him away in order to protect herself and wound up with the opposite outcome.

He was going to be here for her, but he couldn't let himself get close, even if she was an intriguing puzzle. Because he didn't want to know what she would think when she learned the kind of man he really was. A crusader like her would never approve of a guy who didn't measure up.

Mackenzie lifted her chin. "He'll kill you, too."

"You don't know that anything is going to happen to me. You barely know me, which means you can't judge what I'm capable of."

"I've seen you in action. But I'm not going to trust you, not yet. I don't do blind faith in people." She sighed, and a little of the fight in her deflated. "I'll come with you, but my eyes are wide-open."

Aaron studied her. Brown eyes, dull and lonely. Pink lips that should be tipped up in a smile, not dampened with reality. "I can live with that."

Just as long as she didn't see too much, because Aaron would come up short. That was what the women he'd tried to get close to always said. Since the last "it's not you, it's me" conversation, he'd given up. That was three years ago, not that he let the guys on the team know.

Aaron held out his hand, and Mackenzie gave him the first true smile since he'd saved her life yesterday. Why did it feel like so much longer?

He used his grip on her hand to steer her to the truck. It figured that doing Eric a favor meant he had to spend time with a woman who wasn't content with what he was doing for her. No, she had to make it personal, too, and force him to convince her to trust him. She wanted to save him from the danger she posed. He shut the passenger door and rounded the front of the truck, shaking his head.

The sound of engine revs cut through the general hum

of traffic. Aaron looked back in time to see a now-familiar van cut across two lanes of traffic. It was closing in on them fast, ready to ram his truck.

A big engine roared behind them, and Mackenzie turned. It was the van the soldiers had been in. The headlights bore down on them like some macabre scene where a group of kids in a movie watched certain death head straight for them. *So this is how it ends.*

Aaron shoved the key in the ignition. The engine turned over…and over, but didn't catch. The van slammed into the back corner of the truck.

"Go!" Aaron reached past her and flung the door open.

The truck was slammed again until the tires bumped up onto the curb. Aaron shoved her out and followed her, crowding her onto the sidewalk and away from the truck. People screamed and fled in every direction in a haze of panic. Aaron's hand closed around hers as they ran. It was warmer and bigger and imbued her with some of his strength so that she ran faster, harder.

Mackenzie prayed they would be lost in the dispersing crowd. She was dragged along in his wake as he tugged her around the corner, down a back alley.

When she couldn't run anymore she yanked on his hand and bent over. She gasped and sucked in air while Aaron rubbed a firm hand up and down her back.

"Breathe."

"I'm trying." She straightened and took him in. Of course, he wasn't even winded. That must be from his soldier training. "I think I need to work out more. I seriously thought I was in good shape, but apparently that DVD was lying."

He didn't react. Didn't even crack a smile.

"We should get moving."

Mackenzie looked up and down the alley. The Dumpster was overflowing, and the smell of old garbage filled her nose. She took the hand he held out and followed him to where the alley broke onto a busy street, bright with light from restaurants and neon signs.

She sucked in breaths. "Don't you want to know how they found us again so fast? Do you think they're tracking us?"

"I think I'm not going to stand around here and risk catching a disease from all this garbage while we wait for those mercenaries or your Colombian friend to find us." Aaron let go of her hand to curl his arm around her shoulders in a protective gesture.

"He was *never* my friend."

His eyes settled on her. "My mistake."

"Yeah, it is. I didn't ask for this, okay?"

"Wrong place at the wrong time?"

She nodded, because that was essentially true. He watched for a moment at the mouth of the street before he stepped out in time to flag down a cab.

That was it? He had nothing to say? If they'd known for sure Carosa was here, then she could have had a detail of marshals instead of being saddled with Mr. U.S. Army.

Was it too much to ask for a simple conversation? They could get to know each other without her having to tell him everything about Carosa. Aaron had said he wanted to know what happened, but that was only so he could protect her as a favor to his brother. If he didn't have such an obvious devotion to his sibling, Mackenzie would have wondered if he felt anything at all.

Aaron pulled out his phone and hit a bunch of buttons.

Forty-five minutes later, the cab exited the freeway into a residential neighborhood she wouldn't have chosen to be in at this time of night, although to be fair it wasn't much worse than her own street. Small houses. Cars parked on driveways and in the street, bland vehicles that didn't cost much.

Aaron spoke to the driver. "Right here's fine."

They pulled up at a playground covered with graffiti. One of the swings was broken off, leaving two chains dangling. Mackenzie climbed out while he paid the driver and stretched her arms up above her head, trying to relieve the cramp in her muscles. Her legs were shaky and her fingers wouldn't stop trembling. Seriously, she needed a gym membership.

"Jittery?"

She looked over at Aaron.

"It's adrenaline. It'll wear off, but you'll be amped up for a while and then you'll crash as though someone gave you a sleeping pill."

He said it as if that was normal life for him, an everyday occurrence. Had he been on the front lines? Was that how he got injured?

"What is that you do for the army, exactly?" For all she knew, he could be a medic or a cook.

Something flickered in his eyes. "Soldier."

"That's it? That's all you're going to tell me?"

"I'm not allowed to give out specifics, so yeah, that's all I'm going to tell you."

Well, at least he wasn't being curt because it was part of his personality, but that he was actually required to keep it confidential. It seemed as though there was a lot of that going around. They both had enough secrets to fill Madison Square Garden. Would she ever meet anyone who wasn't a federal agent and be able to be completely open with them for a reason other than because it was required of her?

Mackenzie paced a few steps away, trying to burn some

nervous energy, and watched him out the corner of her eye. Did they teach that posture in basic training? His feet were hip-width apart, and his torso was completely still, as though he was waiting for something. The only way she could think to describe it was…ready.

The jitters in her stomach eased. "What are we doing here?"

Aaron folded his arms, the material of his jacket stretched tight. "Waiting for Eric."

"Why is your brother coming here?"

"Because I texted him and asked him to." He sniffed but didn't move otherwise. "The sooner I have all the information about Carosa, the quicker we can get this resolved and I can be done with this vacation. No offense."

That wasn't a problem for her, so long as she wasn't the one who had to say it all out loud. She had no desire to relive any of it.

"Why would I be offended? You just saved my life. Again. And you've agreed to protect me for the time being, right?" He didn't argue. "I wouldn't be standing here if it wasn't for you."

The corner of his mouth twitched. "Uh, you're welcome. I think."

"Doesn't it bother you that you risk your life for your country and you can't even tell anyone about it?"

He shrugged. "Comes with the territory."

"I'm not trying to be mean, or make a judgment about the way you live your life or anything. I'm just trying to figure you out."

Maybe then she could settle herself, find peace with this life of going back and forth between the person she was and the better person she was trying to be. She felt more comfortable in her skin now, but was this truly who she was always supposed to have been?

Aaron frowned. "What's the point? It's not as if we're actually going to be friends."

Mackenzie turned away to hide the flinch. She held back the surge of emotion that felt a lot like right before you burst into tears. Her eyes were hot and her sinuses were about to burst. She might not be ready to trust him fully with her life, but did her concession mean nothing to him? Everything she had—her life, her future—was dependent on him.

She glanced at him now. If she were to allow herself to daydream about what her life could have been, she imagined it might feature someone like him. Strong and courageous, but probably a bit nicer. She could admit that, if only to herself. He was movie-star handsome and probably way out of her league.

If she wasn't in hiding, she could have struck up a conversation that might lead to him asking her out to coffee or dinner and a movie. If she was free to live her life without watching over her shoulder all the time and not wanting to get close to anyone for fear they'd get sucked into this just like—

Don't think about that.

Aaron might be a soldier, but the man she'd thought she was in love with—even if he'd never reciprocated—had been her head of security. And now he was dead.

The man who occupied her thoughts now scanned the road that stretched up the street from where they stood. He ran a hand through his hair, rubbing his head as though he was just as jittery as she was but more familiar with the feeling and better able to dispel it through such a small gesture.

It was a good thing her life wasn't conducive to starting a relationship, because she'd have been hurt by his dismissal. Now she could concentrate on protecting her heart

instead of trying to figure out if there was something behind his insistence on keeping her at arm's length until the
favor was done. That was fine. So long as she was alive
at the end of this. Sure, it would hurt to watch him walk
away, wondering what could have been.

But at least she would be alive to feel it.

SEVEN

Headlights cut a wide arc through the darkness, and then a car pulled up beside them. Mackenzie's breath caught in her throat. When the engine shut off and the driver climbed out, Aaron moved in front of her in a protective gesture. "Eric."

Mackenzie let go of the knot in her stomach and looked at her handler. Eric moved as if he was exhausted. A lot different than the last time she saw him. Was it really just that morning? Now his gray suit was rumpled and his hair looked a month past needing a cut.

When he came within arm's reach, Aaron grabbed Eric by his shirt collar and pulled him so there was an inch of space between their faces. "You seriously look awful."

Eric's lips thinned. "It's been a long day." He gave Mackenzie a small smile. "Was it really just this morning that I was in your office?"

Aaron released him. "I suppose you're not going to tell me what this is, either?"

Eric's blue eyes were a match for Aaron's, except there was something immensely sad there. Apparently satisfied with what he saw, he looked back at Aaron. "Did you get a look at the guys Carosa sent?"

"Mercenaries, probably ex-military. Eight of them. They caught up to us twice."

Mackenzie froze again with the reality that she was being hunted. Even after seeing those guys surround the truck, she was blindsided enough to close her eyes in a futile effort to shut out what was happening. This was her life. Why did it sound so much worse when they said it out loud? The past played like a movie reel in her mind. The burn of pain that felt like ice and fire at the same time, knowing she'd been shot and watching Daniel take his last breath.

Mackenzie stiffened behind him, but he couldn't do anything about it. Eric just stared, while Aaron finally understood why this meant so much to his brother. Why Mackenzie's safety was so important to him, more than just any other witness he was assigned to protect. "Man, I'm so sorry. I'm really sorry, but this doesn't have anything to do with Sarah, does it?"

She shifted again, but Aaron kept still. Eric's fiancée had been tragically injured a year ago, and was now paralyzed from the waist down. Ever since then, Eric seemed to not be able to let go of the need to see Sarah in every woman he met.

Eric shook his head. "It's not like that."

"So you're going to put your job at risk and protect Mackenzie at all costs because you can't let your fiancée go?"

"You think I want to watch Carosa swagger around after exactly the same kind of person who hurt Sarah and killed her family? I won't let anyone else become a victim of selfish people who think they're above the law." Eric's eyes blazed. "I didn't ask you to stay because I can't get over what happened. I asked you to stay because I have to focus on the hunt for the leak, and I don't want to see another woman suffer the way Sarah has."

Eric's fiancée hadn't wanted anything to do with him after the accident. Eric had tried to get her to let him back into her life, but the pain was too great for both of them. In the end he'd had to accept the reality that Sarah wanted it to be over, and move on.

"Um, sorry…but who is Sarah?" Mackenzie's voice was small and more than a little concerned.

Aaron found Mackenzie's hand and gave it a squeeze. "Eric—"

His brother pulled his gaze from Mackenzie back to Aaron. "Outside of you, I don't know who I can trust."

Aaron gave his brother a short nod. Eric needed him, and Aaron wouldn't let anything happen to his brother, his brother's job or anyone else who was innocent and couldn't defend themselves.

He looked at Mackenzie. Her eyes were wide as she took it all in.

"So what now?" Mackenzie asked.

Eric squeezed his eyes shut. "Nothing's changed. Aaron keeps you safe while I find the leak."

Aaron frowned. "Shouldn't you be getting her a new identity and flying her somewhere undisclosed? That's what you guys do, isn't it?"

"If Carosa discovered her location once already, there's nothing to say he can't do it again. And I have to let this internal investigation play out if we're going to find the leak. That's the most likely explanation for what's happening. Regardless of what the police think, it's more likely Carosa hired someone to slash your tires and shoot at you. The mercenaries were probably hired, too, to take you to him so he can get his revenge."

Mackenzie swallowed, her face pale with fear.

Eric continued, "I will get to the bottom of this. It's the only way to keep your identity safe…not to mention anyone else Carosa or the leak decides they want found. This could turn into a bidding war that puts everyone in witness protection in Phoenix in danger."

Mackenzie moved around him to step closer to Eric. "I can help." They both turned to her. "Look, I'm not going to sit around waiting for Carosa to find us again when we could be doing something. I'm not going anywhere and I don't want him hurting anyone else."

Aaron sighed. *So much for giving up.* He kept his eyes on his brother. "We can help you find out who you work with that has a connection to the Carosa cartel. No offense, but you look as if you could use a few extra pairs of hands, and we don't have anything more pressing going on right now."

"The guy's name is Schweitzer." Eric started to shake his head. "But I—"

"Have a team ready to help you?" Aaron studied his brother. "Have a clue who is doing this and a plan to catch them in the act? Have a way to get irrefutable evidence so you can close the file on this quickly and cleanly?" He waited a beat and saw the defeat in his brother's eyes. "Didn't think so."

"Good." Mackenzie squeezed his hand. "Let's make a plan."

Aaron glanced at the woman beside him. Every moment he spent with Mackenzie peeled back another layer of who she was. She might be scared, but she was also dedicated, hardworking, compassionate, wise and unabashedly tenacious.

He needed to keep this about business, take care of things and move on. Between work and his family, Aaron didn't have any room for someone who would sneak into his heart and take up residence before he even realized she was there.

Back when he was dating, it was usually casual, friendly and light enough he could walk away at the end of the evening having had a good time. He'd had no intention of getting involved any deeper, though occasionally it happened naturally.

Mackenzie wasn't like any woman he'd ever spent time with before, which was exactly why he couldn't let her in. Aaron had seen what Sarah's injury did to Eric, what their dad's incarceration had done to his mom. There was no way he was going there. Not when his own mistakes had cost his team so much. His first shot at being team leader, and he was left with an injury while his teammate was forced to retire.

Aaron put his hand on the side of Eric's neck. "Go home and get some sleep. In the morning go to work and do your job. Get us what you can, and I'll take care of this. You have my word I won't let anything happen to Mackenzie."

Because if a good woman was killed, then Aaron would have to right the wrong—a wrong the justice system should have taken care of long before now. And Aaron didn't know if he could take another black mark on his life.

The sound of automatic gunfire rang out across the park. Aaron grabbed Mackenzie with one hand and Eric with the other and hit the sidewalk.

He would really like to know how these guys kept finding them.

"What do we do?"

Mackenzie glanced around from her prone position on the sidewalk. Gravel dug into her hip, but she didn't dare move. The gunfire had stopped. What were they waiting for? Did they really want to take her alive and undamaged like Aaron had said? It seemed more as if they were toying with her so she would freak out. But why would they need her to be unhinged, unless that was part of Carosa's twisted revenge plan?

Nothing about this made any sense.

Eric whipped out his gun. "Mackenzie, get to my car."

Aaron's face was tight, his lips pressed into a thin line. In the yellow light of the streetlamp there was something dark in his eyes. "Both of you, start crawling." He had a gun out, too, and his voice didn't invite any discussion.

Eric's lips thinned. "You go with Mackenzie. I'll take care of the mercenaries."

"No, you go with Mackenzie." Aaron's face invited no argument. "Since I'm the one they're trying to kill, I'm the one who gets to be the diversion."

When Aaron reached the car, he leaned over and spoke to Eric. "On my word, you're going to cover me."

By the look of it, Eric didn't like that idea. "You need to get in the car, too. Get Mackenzie to safety."

"Now. Rendezvous on the north side, but only if it's clear."

Eric fired his gun in rapid succession into the trees. Mackenzie covered her ears. Aaron rushed away and she ducked. Faster gunshots spurted back at them. Eric ducked down also, and shots pinged off the car. "If the mercenaries don't kill him, I will!"

Aaron disappeared behind a bush on the far side of the park, away from the gunfire. That was something, at least. Was it a diversion? She prayed it would work, even if Eric wasn't happy Aaron had made the decision. Minutes later there was a group of gunshots, and then silence.

Mackenzie stuck her elbows out and kept her body to the ground as she moved, like one of those military movies where they crawled through the mud. The asphalt was hot from the day's sun and Eric grunted beside her.

"Shouldn't we call for help?"

"We have to get you to safety first, or we'll be dead before the cops could get here."

She kept moving until she reached the car door, lifted up a fraction and reached for the handle.

"No. Not yet."

She turned to Eric and whispered, "I thought we were going to get out of here."

"We are. But let's give Aaron enough time to draw their attention away."

He watched for a moment. Waited.

"Okay, in the car." Eric opened the door and she crawled across the seat.

"What's happening? Is Aaron dead?"

"No. He's keeping them busy so we can escape. Now get down in the foot well and stay down."

Mackenzie's breath came in snatches. "How do you know he isn't dead?"

"Because those shots we heard were his."

"What now? Are we supposed to pick him up or something?"

"That's what he meant by rendezvous. But only if it doesn't put us in more danger."

Eric started the engine, his body shifted low in the seat. Mackenzie curled up, her body cramped in the small space below the glove box. Aaron had put himself in harm's way so they could escape? She focused on Eric's face as he shot out of the parking lot.

He scanned the area and the rearview mirror and finally said, "Okay, it's clear. You can get up."

Mackenzie crawled onto the seat, feeling the grime of the day and everything that had happened.

Eric motioned behind them. "Your go bag is on the backseat. I stopped by your house and grabbed it for you."

"Thank you." Mackenzie pulled it forward and held it on her knees. She had clean clothes now. Was it selfish to want a shower, too?

She looked around, watching for his return. Aaron was trained for battle, but maybe that didn't work when it was a regular neighborhood.

"Why did he do that?"

Eric glanced at her. "Stay behind?"

She nodded.

"It's what he does."

"As a soldier?" Her brain was spinning with all of it. She wanted to tell him to go back so she could find out if Aaron was okay. They were just going to leave him there?

"Yeah, that, too. But since we were kids he was always that way." Eric flipped on his turn signal and slowed for a stoplight. "Always getting into fights and claiming he slipped. One day he came home covered in mud with a black eye. I was sick with mono or something like that. He said I was faking it just so I could stay home and read comics, but I wasn't. Our foster mom was good, you know? Way better than our real mom."

Mackenzie looked at him. "You were in foster care?"

Eric nodded. "Dad was in jail for armed robbery back then. He's out now, but neither of us are about to make the trip to California just to see him. Mom left us with the neighbor so she could go get high. Couple days later the neighbor called child protective services, and we were placed with Bill and Frankie."

"Wow."

"He's always been the one who took care of... everything. I might have resented it for a while, but that was my issue. I couldn't ask for a better brother than

Aaron, even if he might take it too far sometimes. But I'm making peace with that."

Too far? Eric seemed to think Aaron had done something that he didn't think was a good thing. Both of them seemed so cautious that instead of trusting themselves to others, they retreated to each other every time.

Was it familial love that bound them together? Mackenzie had never known family to be that way. Her parents had walked away the day she joined WITSEC, too enamored with their high-society lifestyle to bother following their daughter into witness protection.

It was a powerful love these two brothers had. Mackenzie could only hope that in her life she'd find someone who would love her that way.

She glanced at Eric. "Thank you for sharing that with me."

Eric gave her a small smile. "There's nothing Aaron wants more in the world than to protect the people he loves."

Mackenzie wanted to know what would happen if feelings were to develop between them. She'd like to think he could feel that way about her, but he held himself back so much she couldn't be sure it was even possible. As soon as Carosa was stopped, Aaron would return to his job with the army and she would go back to her life. They would never see each other again.

In the short time they had left, she wanted to press Aaron and make him open up to her. Not because she liked him, but because the world would be a poorer place if he never loved anyone but his family. Still, if she pushed too far he would likely retreat even further.

Eric turned left and then left again. He stopped at a corner that looked like a different end of the park from where Mackenzie and Aaron had arrived. He tapped his foot, flipping his cell phone over and over in his hand. Then he froze. "There he is."

A figure stepped out of the trees, looked both ways and ran toward them. Aaron slid into the backseat just as two men in black fatigues ran out of the park, pointed their guns at the car and started shooting.

Mackenzie screamed.

Eric gunned the engine and they sped away.

EIGHT

Eric dropped them at a motel just before two o'clock in the morning. It was the kind of place where you paid in cash and no one asked for ID, but at least there was a connecting door between their two rooms that Aaron kept unlocked. As it was, Mackenzie spent most of the night staring at the ceiling. The minute she closed her eyes, she would descend into the world of memory. It happened over and over. Her body would relax enough that she dozed, and shortly after she would wake with a jerk, tangled in the sheets.

She could still hear the gunshots from the park. They had reminded her of that night years ago and the horrible things she'd witnessed. For years after it happened, she had nightmares. The anniversary of that night was always the worst. She would wake up and have to run to the bathroom. Sweating on the floor beside the toilet got old really fast, but thankfully her night hadn't been that bad.

Still, she didn't get any sleep, either.

When sunrise hit the back of the curtains, she got up. Instead of her usual as-fast-as-possible shower, Mackenzie took her time and let the hot water wake her. Her go bag that Eric had brought to the park for her was packed with two spare changes of clothes, extra underwear and shoes. But it was nothing like her WITSEC persona would normally wear. When she opened it, she was filled with a sudden rush of nerves. What if she looked like an idiot?

High fashion might not be her thing now, but it had been once. She couldn't remember the last time she wore jeans with rhinestones—even fake ones. Would she look good, or like a country music wannabe? And who cared anyway, since the only person who was going to see her was Aaron?

She dumped the contents on the bed in a spill of clothes. The jeans had come from a resale store and were prefaded, and the pink top was admittedly cute, but she hadn't had anything that bright in her closet in years. It reminded her of Eva. Was she mad they'd missed dinner?

Hopefully her friend wasn't singlehandedly running the center. But who knew how she was doing? Mackenzie couldn't even call and check. Maybe Chris—the teacher Mackenzie had covered for the first day Aaron was there—was still out with his sick son.

Eva always commented on how she dressed. But Eva just didn't get that, when she was younger, Mackenzie had dressed for the express purpose of drawing attention to herself. Her life now wasn't just about staying below the radar, it was also about not being the person she used to be.

She would probably never be able to tell Eva her story. In fact, something made Mackenzie think she might never see her friend again. Eric would set her up with a new identity in some half-empty state where she could live in the mountains in seclusion, hiding from Carosa for the rest of her life. Aaron was no doubt a skilled soldier, but would he be able to go up against a drug cartel?

Mackenzie wanted to scream. Just walk outside, look up at the sky and shriek until she had no breath left. She would surely be alone and hiding for the rest of her life. But she would still do it, because it was the small bit of power she had left.

She wanted to hold on to what she could control for a little bit longer—long enough to balance the scales.

When his friend's sedan pulled up outside, Aaron stepped out of his motel room into the dry heat of eight o'clock in the morning. Hours had passed since they'd been shot at, but he could still hear it ringing in his ears. He needed reinforcements and was glad he'd been able to reach Sabine Laduca last night. His former team leader's fiancée was a former CIA agent. If anyone could help, it was Sabine.

Sabine's smile was wide as she stepped out of the car, and if he'd been able to see her eyes behind the huge sunglasses she wore, there would probably be a gleam of mischief there.

"You look a little rough this morning."

He snorted. "I'm thinking that's an understatement."

"Bad night?"

"You could call it that, yeah. I liked the automatic weapons especially."

Sabine pushed her sunglasses to the top of her head, her eyes wide. It hadn't been that long since she'd been branded a rogue CIA agent and became the subject of a manhunt while she searched for her brother's killer. Ben—Sabine's brother and Aaron's former teammate—had been killed in action, but it was a hit that was paid for. Ben had been murdered by Sabine's mom.

It had taken the whole team working, and especially Aaron's former team leader, Doug, to get her out of that fix. But now her mom was dead, and Sabine had Doug's ring on her finger.

"Enough of that, though." Aaron grinned. "Mademoiselle."

Sabine laughed and gave him a quick one-armed hug. "Yeah, yeah. Cut it out, I'm an engaged woman."

"Doesn't make you any less beautiful." Aaron said it without thinking, but it hit home. She looked happy. And the way she looked at Doug? Aaron's former team leader was a fortunate guy. But Doug would say it was God's blessing.

As a kid, Aaron had gone to church. After all, it was part of the deal he'd struck with his foster parents. Still, he didn't see how God had done anything much for him, let alone bless him. That was why he'd left faith behind when he went into the army. And he'd done fine without it, so why change things now, simply because his friend had some kind of revelation?

Aaron motioned to the car. "What do you have for me?"

"One staid, boring, completely unnoticeable car bought with cash. The plates are still registered to the dealership until we do the paperwork."

"Great, thanks."

Sabine's gaze flicked to the motel room beside his. "So what's she like, this Mackenzie Winters?"

Aaron narrowed his eyes. "What do you think you know?"

"Nothing. I didn't even do a full computer search or anything. You should be proud of me."

He wanted to roll his eyes, but let her have her moment. She could find out just about anything if she wanted to. Maybe not that Mackenzie was in WITSEC, but Sabine could likely make a good guess if she uncovered enough evidence that suggested Mackenzie's identity had been constructed instead of lived. She had been trained by the CIA after all.

Sabine smiled. "It's a great thing she's doing, with those kids at the center. Only…I'm just curious why she needs protecting? I can guess since you told me your brother, the U.S. Marshal is involved, but I wouldn't want to assume."

"Good. Let's keep it that way." Of course she would figure it out. He should never have told her this had to do with Eric. "We'll be fine, Sabine. I've got this covered."

"I know you do. It's just…with Doug in Tampa talking to that guy about a job—" Aaron had talked to Doug before he left town about the interview. His former team leader was still looking for work that would suit him as well as the army had.

"I'm kind of—" she came close and whispered, as if it was a secret "—bored."

"Wedding planning isn't turning out to be as exciting as you thought?"

Sabine laughed. "No, it's not that at all. I mean, it's going to be great getting married and then being married. But this seems interesting, too." She waved her hand, encompassing him and the motel rooms. "It could be fun."

"Sure, running for your life when people are shooting at you is great fun."

Sabine rolled her eyes. "You don't have to say it like that."

"And if I let you get shot at while Doug was out of town, what then?"

She sighed. "Fine. I'll go back to tulle and sequins and vol-au-vents."

A cab pulled up in the parking lot and Sabine held up one finger to the driver. "But if you need anything, and I mean *anything,* you give me a call, okay?"

Aaron held on to the laughter that wanted to spill out. "Sure, Sabine. I'll do that."

At the knock, Mackenzie stood up from the bed with her shoes tied but didn't cross the room. "Who is it?" As if she didn't know. She'd seen Aaron out front talking to a glamorously beautiful woman fifteen minutes ago, before the shower went on in his room. Of course he was in a relationship. Aaron was a good-looking man, and he could be nice enough…when he wanted.

Mackenzie pushed away the ridiculous feeling of disappointment and looked through the peephole.

"It's me."

She rolled her eyes and opened the door. Aaron stood there with one hand high on the door frame looking more casual than she'd ever felt in her life. He wore designer jeans and a collared T-shirt with three buttons. How did he manage to look like a movie star when his hair was still mussed from sleep? She probably had bags under her eyes.

He smiled. "Ready to go?"

"Where did you get a change of clothes from?"

"I ordered them."

"From that woman who was here?" Mackenzie's sleep-deprived brain made her mouth blurt it out before she could catch it. "Never mind. It's none of my business."

"Her name is Sabine."

So she had a cool name. That didn't mean Mackenzie had to like her, or the way she smiled at Aaron as if they were best pals. "Are we coming back? Should I bring my bag?"

"Pack it and carry it with you. I'm not sure if we're coming back, so it's better to hold on to everything since it's not much anyway."

Mackenzie crammed her things in her bag and zipped it closed. "Where are we headed?"

He was frowning at her. "I figured breakfast, for starters."

She ignored his obvious need for her to explain why she was in a bad mood and said, "Great, I'm starving. Is there somewhere within walking distance?"

He motioned over his shoulder. "Made a call last night

and procured us a new ride that Sabine brought, along with clothes. The car is untraceable, so we'll be able to stay off the radar of anyone trying to find us." His eyes studied her. "But a walk actually sounds good. There's a diner around the corner."

Mackenzie hesitated. "Am I supposed to know what that means, you 'procured us a ride' or should I just not ask?"

He shrugged. "Means what it means. I didn't want to leave you unprotected, so I needed the stuff brought to me. I made a call and got it done."

Mackenzie couldn't help it. She had to ask, even if that made her weak and needy. "So who is Sabine? Other than someone who will drop everything just because you called and show up before breakfast with a car that no one can trace and some clothes."

And didn't that just burn a little. Mackenzie was a nice person, wasn't she? There must be some other reason she didn't have friends like that. Perhaps she had been such an awful person in the past that it showed through now. Or this was yet more punishment.

Maybe everyone in WITSEC felt this alone, a pariah who couldn't seem to make friends. Mackenzie had to hide every single thing she was actually good at, holding it at arm's length while she pushed papers and tried to convince herself she was doing something worthwhile.

"You really want to know about Sabine?"

"Am I not allowed? Is that something we're not supposed to talk about?"

He sighed. "Mackenzie. You're making this a bigger deal than it needs to be. She's just a friend, who is actually more the fiancée of a friend of mine. Sabine had some troubles a while back. I worked with her brother when he was killed, and my team leader then, Doug, helped her with her problem and they fell in love."

"Right." Mackenzie slung the bag over one shoulder. "Lead the way, then."

So she wasn't his girlfriend, but he still probably had someone special in his life. There was no way a guy who looked like he did was available. Unless there was something wrong with him.

She'd met enough good-looking people in her former life to know they often didn't have character to match. And while he didn't seem completely as though he thought the world revolved around him, he definitely possessed an air of authority—the kind that assumed you'd either hop along for the ride or leave.

Aaron grabbed her backpack and they walked by the faded gray car parked in front of their motel rooms. He glanced at her. "You look great, by the way."

Maybe that was his idea of an apology. She looked down at the clothes she had packed. "Not exactly my style." She might actually blend in with women her age for once, instead of looking like a librarian spinster.

"Still." Aaron held the door to the diner open for her. "You look nice."

The chain diner was one she only went to every few months when the need for carbs overwhelmed the desire not to eat a thousand calories in one sitting. They found an open booth, and she studied the options, trying to convince herself she was going to be strong and get the fruit and oatmeal. She let the plastic menu drop. Maybe it was best to accept the inevitable.

A voluptuous waitress poured coffee for them, and Mackenzie shot her a smile. "I need biscuits and gravy."

Aaron nodded. "What the lady wants, she shall have."

The waitress leaned in toward Mackenzie. "You've got to love a man with that attitude."

Aaron laughed, and the waitress walked away smiling.

Mackenzie squinted at him and crossed her arms on the table. "Why are you in such a good mood all of a sudden?"

"I can't be happy?"

"It's just weird. You bump into my life—literally—and all of a sudden you're a mainstay. You never really talk to me except to tell me what to do. You're in my business and being my protector. Not that I'm not grateful. And now I'm supposed to share all my secrets?"

A smile played on his lips. "You might want to take a breath."

She sighed. "Now what? You want to be friends or something?"

Aaron's eyes widened, and he took a sip of his coffee. When he replaced his cup on the table, he looked up at her. "There's nothing wrong with making this whole thing more enjoyable by being pleasant to one another."

Mackenzie stared at him. "Who are you?"

Aaron tipped his head back and laughed. Mackenzie just sat there. It was as though the stress of the past two days had been wiped away and they were just two people sharing breakfast.

It was great for him that he could push it aside, but she wasn't wired that way. Nor was she convinced this would ever be over for her or that she'd come to a point when she wasn't running from Carosa. Or a bunch of mercenaries who seemed to be able to show up everywhere they went.

He cleared his throat. "Seriously, though, this will be a whole lot more pleasant if we get along."

"So tell me about yourself, then. What is your job like? Did you get injured on a mission? Is that what you're recovering from?"

"Yeah, it was a work injury." He didn't say any more, just reached for his cup and took another sip.

Mackenzie took a chance on a different but not less sensitive subject. "Who was Sarah?"

He blinked. "Eric's Sarah?"

"He mentioned her last night. It sounded as if something happened to her. Was she killed?" Mackenzie swallowed. "Will you tell me what happened?"

NINE

Aaron would have much rather gone back to the light-hearted banter, or Mackenzie trying to discern whether or not he was in a relationship—which was interesting in itself.

The waitress delivered his skillet with everything and Mackenzie's biscuits and gravy.

The woman across the table was a pretty good distraction with those different clothes on, but she still had her hair in that awful bun that made her face look pinched. Whatever it took to convince him that he wasn't drawn to her, he had to focus on that.

When this was done, she would find someone else, and Aaron would go back to being single and trying to repair the damage he'd done to his career. And his friend's life.

He set his fork down. He should probably get on with the story.

"Sarah was…Sarah. Beautiful. Smart, like crazy smart. She was an accountant when she met Eric and they started dating, but after they got engaged she fell in with the wrong people before he could stop it. Then they had her trapped with threats to her mom and dad. Eric had her contact the FBI, but they couldn't get the evidence for more than surveillance and definitely not enough to get her, or her parents, in witness protection.

"Eric set her parents up so they could disappear, and she went back to work, under cover of the FBI. She handed the feds everything she could about how her employers forced her to launder money for them. Eric didn't like it, but figured the FBI would keep her safe. Aside from them running, too, there wasn't much else they could do."

Aaron glanced at the room of diners but didn't really see any of them. "Sarah discovered that what she knew was just the tip of things. You could make a case that she got cocky and pushed it too far so they made a move to kill her, but the fact is both she and her parents were gunned down in a supposedly random drive-by. As if no one would see the correlation. Sarah was paralyzed and her parents were killed. Eric is convinced someone at the FBI leaked the fact that she was working for them and her employers retaliated. It's just too big of a coincidence to be anything else."

"That must have taken a lot of guts, for her to do that."

"What it was is stupid."

Mackenzie gasped. "How can you say that? She did the right thing, trying to bring criminals to justice."

"Might have been right, but it wasn't smart. Now her parents are dead, and my brother doesn't trust anyone because she pushed him away."

Mackenzie frowned. "You don't think there's a mole?"

He shrugged. "Maybe there is, maybe there isn't. It doesn't mean it has anything to do with you. I'm not big on coincidences, but it doesn't totally fit. Unless it's a smoke screen to cover someone helping Carosa. Either way, if it puts you in danger then we have a problem, because there's more than just Carosa and his mercenaries to worry about, and that's enough by itself."

"What if we could find out?"

Aaron studied her. "Eric got to you."

"So what if he did? He lost the relationship he had with the woman he loved and I feel for him, which means I have a heart. He might be barking up the wrong tree—"

"Let's just call it what it is. Paranoia."

"Still, even if he's just grieving the loss of his relationship and—"

"Unhinged?"

"You really think that? Explain to me what's wrong about helping him make sense of all this."

Aaron swallowed the last bite of his eggs and tossed his fork on the plate with a clatter. "Those kids at that center of yours aren't enough of a crusade—you have to take up Eric's cause, too?"

Why did she need to save everyone? He didn't even understand it. She was practically an alien species. It was a good thing he didn't have his own crusade, or she'd probably take that on, as well.

Mackenzie flinched. "Since when did helping people become a bad thing?"

"I didn't say it was. But if it consumes your whole life because all you're doing is using up your energy fighting for other people's causes, then how is that good?"

"Because they need me."

Aaron covered her hand with his. "I'm just saying you might not be doing them a favor if all you're doing is killing yourself in the process."

"That's my choice."

"But why would you choose that?"

She pulled her hand out from under his. "That's none of your business."

"Maybe I'm making it my business."

Her eyes went wide. "What does that mean?"

"I'm not going to protect you so you can go kill yourself trying to save everyone else. If we're going to help Eric, we do it my way, because you seriously have no idea what you're getting into."

"Wow, thanks. That's so flattering." Her mouth flattened into a sneer. "You need my help, oh, poor defenseless female, because you don't know how to do anything except teach people how to sing, and you don't even do that because you hide in the office all day."

Aaron ran his hand through his hair. "I didn't mean it like that, okay? You have plenty of skills. Unfortunately, none of them have anything to do with covert investigation into a federal agency. Which the FBI is already doing, I might add."

Her head cocked to one side. "And you do?"

"Actually, yeah."

She didn't relax, still energized with anger. "What do you do?"

He really wasn't supposed to tell her. But if a woman in WITSEC couldn't keep a secret, who could? And she needed to know he could do this. "I already told you I'm a sergeant in the army. My unit is small and specializes in missions that require stealth and finesse."

"Like James Bond?"

"That would be espionage. We're talking about soldiers."

"Special soldiers."

He grinned. "I like to think so."

"Like Special Forces?"

"I'm not going to lie, it is specialized work. For the purposes of protecting you, you can know at least that much. We train constantly when we're not on missions just so that we stay sharp. Each of my team knows the other's movements like their own. They have to, or one of us could misjudge something and end up getting killed."

"And do they all have big egos like you do?"

He laughed. "Definitely. We work extremely hard to be the best. You can't afford to be average. That's how people get dead."

Aaron waited while she processed this information. She'd known him as a bodyguard and soldier, an average guy. Not to mention there was a disconnect between sitting in a diner and what she likely knew of covert ops from movies and TV.

After a minute or so of her opening her mouth but saying nothing, he smiled. "Feel better now that you know?"

There might be more to the story, since he'd have to fight to regain his standing within the team. But, his disastrous debut as leader notwithstanding, Mackenzie needed to know he was capable of protecting her from Carosa. He might have messed everything up, but he wasn't going to let anything happen to her.

Mackenzie frowned. "I guess. I mean, there are worse people to have protecting you than a Special Forces soldier, I suppose."

"Uh, thanks." Apparently she didn't get the significance of what he'd just told her. It was a huge thing in his world for someone to know what they did for a living. Delta Force wasn't just a job, it was their lives. And keeping it a secret meant everything.

Together they walked to the front door of the restaurant, where he held the door open for her.

"Do we have somewhere to be now?"

Aaron saw the fatigue in her eyes. "No. I think we both need a breather for the rest of today. After we check ourselves out, we can drive and find a new motel, get some rest, hole up for a few days somewhere quiet."

Long enough for him to look into Eric's coworkers, specifically the man he'd mentioned, Schweitzer. And maybe long enough for Aaron to find out how Carosa's mercenaries had found them twice now. Long enough to get some distance from a woman who smelled like whipped cream and sunshine.

She frowned. "Didn't we push it by hanging out here and getting breakfast?"

And miss the most important meal of the day? "Gotta eat somewhere. But it's probably a good idea to keep moving rather than risk being found. They do seem to have a knack for locating us."

She looked around.

"Everything's going to be fine, okay?"

"Sure," she said. But she didn't sound as if she believed him.

He waited while she let herself into her room. She strode to the bathroom, pulled back the shower curtain and then came out and looked under the bed.

"Checking for bad guys? I thought that was my job."

Mackenzie straightened. "No, I was just making sure I hadn't forgotten my shampoo, or a sock, or something."

Aaron smiled. "Gotcha."

Wheels screeched to a halt outside. Aaron pulled back the curtain an inch. A now-familiar black van was parked out front. "Time to go."

"How do we get out of here?"

A fist pounded on the door. "We know you're in there. Come out, or we let ourselves in!"

Aaron pulled out his sidearm. "Bathroom window. Now."

Mackenzie swung her backpack over her shoulder and strode to the bathroom. He crowded in behind her and shut the door.

Mackenzie turned back, wide-eyed. "I don't think it opens."

"It will." He moved her aside and shielded her with his body while he used the butt of the gun to shatter the frosted glass of the tiny bathroom window. Then he knocked out the remaining shards.

He heard the front door hit the wall and hauled Mackenzie toward the window, ignoring her shriek. "Go!"

The bathroom door flew open and a small canister rolled into the room. Aaron spun Mackenzie and stuck her face in his shoulder, covering her head with his arms while he squeezed his eyes shut as the flash bang went off.

He went for the window again to the sound of boots stomping through the room and calls of "Clear!"

Mackenzie gripped his arm, her other hand grasping a handful of Aaron's shirt. She was ready to move, but a surge of men wearing black fatigues and carrying AR-15s stormed in. All the weapons were pointed at Aaron. He forced his fingers to still and not reach for his gun.

One of the men spoke. "Lani Anders, you need to come with us."

Lani Anders? The image of a teenage star dressed to look like an adult flashed in his mind, but Aaron didn't have time to process the name and what that meant about Mackenzie and the girl she'd been so many years ago.

How was he supposed to get them out of this? He only had a handgun and Mackenzie gripping the back of his shirt, trusting him not to let her down. Fear was a foreign feeling and one he wasn't sure he liked at all.

Aaron stared them down, four men from the park. Guns for hire—that was never good. Although the fact they only worked for the money they made might be his doorway in.

He focused on the point man. "Whatever you're being paid, I'll give you double to walk out the door right now."

The mercenary's eyes flicked to Aaron. "Think not, dude."

Another of the hired guns pulled on Mackenzie's arm. "Walk or we kill you both."

TEN

Mackenzie whimpered, not taking her eyes from him—as though pleading with him to do something. Was he supposed to burst into motion and save them, against four guys with automatic weapons? No one was that good in real life, just in movies.

The fear in her eyes churned his stomach. They were mercenaries; they wouldn't get paid if she wasn't delivered—intact.

She was pulled away. A tear rolled down her face. He wanted to reach for her, and not just because he was there to protect her and failure would be awkward to explain to his brother. He'd spent breakfast looking at her across the table, seeing her smile. And now he really didn't want to lose her.

"Aaron..." His name was a low, keening cry. But he couldn't do anything.

Didn't she know any move he made would lead to him being killed and maybe even her, too? He didn't mind taking risks with his own life, but he wasn't about to lose her. That would be a lousy end to his vacation.

"Move, woman. Now."

Aaron gritted his teeth at the steroid-induced soldier talk. What was with this Neanderthal? Mackenzie didn't release her grip on Aaron's arm. He moved an inch. A gun muzzle swung to him and stopped a hairsbreadth from the end of his nose. "I've warned you already. You wanna get dead?"

Aaron shook his head a fraction. "You've got no problem from me."

His hands curled into fists. They weren't going to kill her. They were going to take her to Carosa, and Aaron was going to run them down and get Mackenzie back—if she would just let go of his arm.

The mercenary turned to her. "You get to walking or I make a hole in your man's head."

She released Aaron's arm immediately. It was the right thing. He couldn't lose her. And maybe in the process of getting her back he could get a lead on Carosa, or find out if there really was a leak in the Marshals Service.

The minute they were out the door he'd be after them, jumping in his car and gunning the engine in pursuit. One last flash of hurt in Mackenzie's eyes and she was out the door, surrounded by three mercenaries like a Secret Service detail. Aaron stood fast, waiting for his chance to go after her.

The gun butt came out of nowhere. Pain drummed through his temple and everything went black.

Mackenzie clenched her jaw to keep her teeth from chattering. The plastic tie she was bound with was thin and cut into her wrists. Her arms were pulled back, making her shoulders feel as if they were on fire. Tears filled her eyes, but she held them at bay, not wanting four macho men to see her break down.

He'd just stood there and let her go.

Now she knew what kind of man Aaron was—the kind who didn't come through for you when it really counted.

He'd let the soldiers take her to Carosa to die. What a fool she'd been to trust him, to believe that he would keep her safe when he only cared about protecting his brother's reputation. Had this been his plan all along? Wait for the first opportunity and then hand her over and walk away?

Mackenzie shuddered as icy tendrils of fear crept through her.

The van raced west along Interstate 10. What if he was just a car or two behind them? Maybe he really did care about her safety. That was possible, right? Maybe he'd wanted her to get caught so he could find Carosa. But then what? She squeezed her eyes shut. There was no one else in the world she wanted to rescue her. Just Aaron.

They turned left and she saw a sign for a small municipal airport.

Mackenzie looked back, but no one took the turn to the gate behind them. Aaron's car was nowhere in sight. He'd let her go, and if there was any hope for her, she was going to have to make it herself.

The van was waved through security and drove between two hangars onto the tarmac where a small plane was waiting. Tears ran down her cheeks. Here, little more than one hundred and fifty miles from the Mexican border, Mackenzie faced the fact she would never have the chance to say goodbye to any of the center kids or Eva.

She would be in Carosa's hands, dead in a fit of revenge. Killed by a man who thought saving face for his family—killing the woman he thought had brought the cartel low—was more important than life.

Aaron came around on the carpet of the motel. His arms were bound behind him, so he arched his back and slipped his feet between his elbows, bringing his arms to the front and almost kneeing himself in the face in the process. *Ouch*. Then he lay back on the floor and sucked in air, trying not to black out while his shoulder screamed with pain.

Lani Anders.

It was almost unreal. It didn't make any sense at all that Mackenzie was the same girl who danced and sung in packed arenas all those years ago. Aaron had been in the early days of basic training then, and after that came his first posting—to Georgia. Lani had been all over the magazines and radio, her songs heard everywhere.

He pulled out his phone and made a call from the motel floor.

Eric answered on the second ring. "What's up, brother?"

Aaron sniffed, pushing away the throb. "Well, I'm tied up for starters. They got Mackenzie. Or, I should say, former teen superstar *Lani Anders*."

Eric muttered something Aaron didn't catch and then said, "Where are you?"

"Lying on the floor in—"

"Well, get up. Go after her."

"The guy clocked me with his weapon. Give me a second, and quit shouting." Aaron sat up and focused on his boot laces. "Four mercenaries in a black van. It's really starting to make me angry how they seem to be able to find us everywhere we go."

"What? How?"

"Exactly. On the way to the restaurant, at the park and now at the motel. It's been barely twelve hours since the last attack and they show up. *Again*. They have to be tracking us. There's no other explanation."

Aaron got to his feet and swayed a little. Once he was sitting in his car he'd be okay. If he could find his knife and cut the ties on his hands. "I have to get going. Any idea how to track a van without letting anyone know we're tracking it?"

Eric sighed. "Why don't you call Sabine?"

"I can't, man. Doug will kill me if I involve her more than I already have."

It was true. His former team leader wouldn't want Sabine involved, even if she was an ex-spy. And for a teen pop star who'd used her looks to get what she wanted? The mental picture of Lani Anders juxtaposed with Mackenzie's face, scared and being taken away... Aaron couldn't get it to fit. No wonder she hadn't wanted to tell him.

Eric said, "Never mind Doug, I'll kill you if you let Mackenzie get hurt, and Sabine will kill you if she finds out you're in trouble and didn't call her. Didn't she help you get that car?"

Aaron found his backpack and pulled out the multitool his brother had sent him for Christmas. It took some doing, but he got the knife out and sawed through his bonds. "I'll give her a call."

Mackenzie was shuffled out of the van by the combined motion of two big men, which was sort of helpful since her hands were tied in front of her. They just moved and she got caught up in the wave. She stumbled finding her feet, her hands slamming on the ground. Her knee hit the asphalt and pain shot to her hip, but no one came to her assistance. One of the soldiers in front turned to see what was happening and waited while she stood up.

Apparently it didn't matter if she was a little damaged upon delivery.

They walked her across the tarmac toward the plane. The horizon was a haze of heat coming up from the runway. An aircraft took off behind them in a rush of engine noise and wind that whipped her hair across her face.

Mackenzie shuffled along, dragging it out, trying to make it take as long as possible to get to the plane. Once she was on board, they would be gone and Aaron would have to search longer and harder for her.

If he even intended to.

She scanned the area. It was too open to run. They would either shoot her or chase her down in no time. But what other choice did she have? She'd been pretty good at track before she quit high school to go on the road full time. Maybe sneakers and none of that heavy stuff they carried on their belts—and the fact they didn't seem interested in killing her right here—meant she might have a chance to get away.

The front end of a gun poked at her back and she continued her steady forward shuffle pretending she didn't feel well. Good thing she didn't have to feign anything. The knee she'd fallen on stung and her jeans were starting to stick. Was she bleeding?

Aaron wasn't coming. He knew who he'd been protecting. Maybe that was why he wasn't coming. Maybe he'd decided she wasn't worth it.

Quit feeling sorry for yourself. You need to get away from these guys.

Car tires screeched as a vehicle wound a semicircle in front of them, cutting off their forward progress. Mackenzie shrieked and the men dived out of the way. She pushed away the question of whether it was smart or not and tore across the stretch of runway to the nearest building. She pumped her legs over and over, ignoring the sting in her knee and thinking only of safety and freedom. Her bound hands were no help, so she tucked her elbows close to her body and kept going.

Gunfire erupted, followed by the ping of metal hitting metal. Had someone called her name? She crossed the threshold of a hangar and plunged into darkness. Her footsteps faltered, and she slowed down enough so she could hear her pursuers.

They were gaining on her.

Mackenzie picked her way deeper into the hangar, angling toward the outside wall so she could get her bearings. Should she have stopped by the door and ducked to one side? Should she just freeze in the dark in the hope they wouldn't be able to find her? Why was she no good at this?

Flashlight beams swept the room.

Mackenzie ran for the door at the back.

"There she is. Two o'clock."

Bullets whizzed past her. Apparently when someone ran, they were fair game to be shot.

A thump was followed by the spurt of more bullets, but these weren't directed at her. Another thump. Mackenzie twisted the handle and barreled through the door. It was an office with a metal desk, a file cabinet and absolutely no exit. She closed herself in, heart pounding in her chest and her lungs screaming for air.

The blood in her hands throbbed. She needed to cut them lose, so she felt her way backward to the desk drawer and found a pair of scissors. She nearly dislocated her thumb, but she cut the tie and her hands were finally free.

Flexing her fingers and shoulders, she ignored the pins and needles rushing through her skin and went for the window. She pushed and shoved at the frame, waiting for someone to come in. Waiting for gunfire.

For death.

ELEVEN

The window wouldn't open. Again, Mackenzie sank to the floor. Tears filled her eyes. Someone had caused a diversion, subdued her captors and then…left. What kind of person did that? But honestly, she shouldn't expect more. She'd been alone forever. There were hundreds, if not thousands of people in witness protection.

Sarah had been hurt simply because she did the right thing, while Mackenzie worked a job she adored and got to feel every day as though she was making a difference. Until it all fell apart. If Eric's fiancée hadn't been saved from harm, what made Mackenzie think she was good enough to be rescued?

Salty tears touched her lips. She swiped away the wetness from her cheeks, tucked her chin to her knees and squeezed herself as tight as possible. She hadn't asked for this. It was a high price to pay for being self-absorbed—too high. Daniel, her head of security, was dead. Her manager was dead, too, and she was all alone in the dark waiting for Carosa to kill her. Other people got to live their lives, but she was being punished for the way she'd been.

Why, Lord? This is too hard. I can't do it. Take it away, please.

She sobbed into her hands, sucking in breaths and trying to get air. The doorknob rattled, and Aaron was there. "Mackenzie. Thank God I found you."

She burst into tears again.

Aaron crossed the room and gathered her in his arms. "They're gone. You're okay."

She squeezed her eyes shut and soaked in the feel of him holding her. "I don't think that's true. I don't think I'm okay." He was really here? "You're here. You came."

"Of course I came. You think I'd let Carosa get you?"

"You let them take me from the motel."

"I couldn't incapacitate four of them all by myself. I had to turn the situation in my favor if I had any hope of getting you back."

"By letting me walk away?"

His hands moved to the sides of her face and his thumbs wiped the tears from her face. Even in the dark she could see the softness in his eyes. "I came, didn't I? Can't that be enough?"

Mackenzie bit her lip. "You don't hate me because I didn't tell you…about me being Lani?"

"Of course not. It threw me, but I get that you didn't want to cloud my judgment of who you are."

Mackenzie closed her eyes and sucked in a breath. She didn't deserve what he was doing for her. Not when she was a liar. Despite the look of concern in his eyes, a look that said he was sorry for the pain he'd caused her, it didn't matter who she was now.

Part of her would always be that selfish girl who had thought she ruled the world. She didn't deserve someone who could brush aside all the wrong she'd done as though it was no big deal. It was too big to pass off as forgivable.

Aaron's warm hands moved down to gently squeeze her shoulders. Mackenzie opened her eyes in time to see him tilt his head to the side, and she knew what was coming…

Until he stood and backed away, and then ran a hand through his hair.

Had he actually been about to kiss her? Mackenzie tried to tell herself that wasn't what she wanted. She needed time—time to get herself together and figure out why all this was happening. Why did her past have to come back now? Why couldn't she still be at the center, doing the good that she was supposed to be doing? There was no way she could make up for any of it if she was alone with Aaron, running from Carosa.

Always running.

The air between them was cold, so she wrapped her arms tight around herself, not willing to give in to the shudders. He might say he understood, but eventually he would see Lani when he looked at her. It was inevitable.

"Are you two going to stay there all day, or can we get out of here?"

Mackenzie looked beyond Aaron to the door of the warehouse office. The glamorous woman from the motel stood there with one hand on her hip.

"You're telling me I was only in there for ten minutes?"

Sabine turned back from the front passenger seat of her rental car and squeezed Mackenzie's hand. "Felt like much longer, didn't it?"

Mackenzie nodded, unable to believe she spent such a short time alone in the hangar's office. It seemed like so much longer before Aaron walked her out and introduced the woman as Sabine, his former team leader's fiancée.

Sabine had laughed and added, "Ex-CIA. For a while now, since my mom—who was an international arms dealer and all-around criminal—duped me into running missions for her. Until she killed my brother and tried to kill me, too. Doug helped me. My mom didn't survive, but we did. Now Doug and I are getting married."

Mackenzie liked her. "How did you find me?"

"Uh...well, I had the cab drop me at the rental place and doubled back to the motel. I saw you guys return from breakfast. When the mercenaries took you but not Aaron, I followed."

Mackenzie laughed. "Why did you say that as though you've done something you shouldn't have? You saved me." She seemed so perfect, while Mackenzie was the kid who got picked on in P.E.

"Aaron told me to leave it alone." Sabine rolled her eyes. "He should know me better than that."

"Have you been friends long?"

Sabine nodded and some of the levity disappeared from her eyes. "My brother was on the team with Doug and Aaron. I've hung out with all of them when they were home a bunch of times, but only really got to know the rest of the guys since Doug, even though he's no longer on the team." Her smile turned wistful.

"I'm sorry you lost your brother."

Sabine gave her a small smile. "Thank you, Mackenzie."

Mackenzie kept her eyes on Sabine so she wasn't tempted to look out the front window of the car, at Aaron. Again. Sabine hadn't asked, she'd just handed him her keys and he drove them, since he didn't want to keep the other car any longer. Sabine had tried to get Mackenzie to ride up front, but it would've been too weird.

After he parked them behind a warehouse in an industrial district he excused himself and got out to use his phone. It might make her feel better if he'd even looked her in the eye once since he hadn't almost tried to kiss her in the warehouse.

Why was he being so weird about it? So she'd jumped to

the wrong conclusion about why he was getting close and he didn't feel anything romantic for her. Couldn't they just forget about her monumental dorkiness thinking he really was about to kiss her and move past this awkwardness?

Mackenzie sighed. "So you were the one driving the car? You provided the distraction so I could run away from those men?"

"Except you were supposed to get in, not run away."

Mackenzie's stomach churned with a combination of lingering adrenaline and embarrassment.

"That was when Aaron showed up in the car I left you guys." Sabine smiled. "Time seems to stretch itself out when you're hiding, overwhelmed by fear."

Mackenzie rolled her eyes. She didn't want to be that weak woman, but there was just so much to be afraid of. "That makes me sound stupid." She glanced out the window where Aaron paced back and forth by the building, talking on his phone with big hand motions and a tight face. "I don't like being overcome by fear. Helpless."

"We've all been there. Me, plenty of times. No one thinks any less of you, least of all Aaron."

Mackenzie frowned. "He's a soldier. I doubt he understands hiding in the dark and crying because you're scared someone's going to kill you."

"On the contrary." Sabine's face gentled. "Soldiers probably understand fear better than any of us, but the job they do means they have to channel that fear into completing the mission. Fear is good. It keeps you sharp."

"That sounds a lot like personal experience."

Sabine's nose crinkled. "It is. The CIA thought I was a traitor and my mom, of all people, was trying to kill me. But haven't you had to overcome your fair share of fear? Performing in front of thousands of screaming fans can't

have been easy. How did you overcome your nerves then?"
She bit her lip. "I hope you don't mind, but Aaron told me."

She shrugged one shoulder. Mackenzie had never even
thought of fame like that. "It's true. I did get really nervous, especially before those big shows. I don't think you
ever get used to it, and the attention was just part of what
made up that lifestyle."

"So how did you deal with it?"

"You just push it aside and get on with it, I guess."
Mackenzie laughed. "Boy, I never would have thought
fighting stage fright would apply to running for your life
from men with guns."

"You have the tools already, Mackenzie. Almost as
though God knew one day you might need them."

She glanced out the window again but couldn't see
Aaron. "What about Aaron…and your fiancé? What makes
them put themselves in harm's way on purpose?"

"It's the kind of men they are, I suppose. Highly specialized skills and a personality that means they can risk
their lives on a daily basis and never get any credit for it
because no one even knows that's what they do for a living. And they'll get up and do it all again tomorrow."

Aaron was so relaxed about his life. Everything except
for Eric seemed as if it wasn't a big deal to him, even being
Special Forces. She was sure it was his job that showed
him what was really important. After all, he had given up
his time to help Eric, even though he was injured.

How would it feel if he turned that commitment and loyalty to her? There was no doubt that whomever he fell for
would be a blessed woman. Maybe it would be her, maybe
not. And why did that make her want to kick something?

She didn't even know if Mackenzie Winters was the
kind of girl who fell in love. Her WITSEC persona might
feel more real, but even after all these years sometimes

she still had to think what the girl she was now would do. Besides, she was too busy with the center for romance. Or, that was what she'd always thought.

But then, maybe there was more to her that she hadn't let grow because she'd been so busy trying to be the best Christian she could be. Her life the past sixteen years had been so narrow, her world so isolated, that it was hard to believe she could ever be truly normal.

How could a romantic relationship help balance the scales of the person she'd been? When would she feel like she'd finally atoned for being a shallow, self-centered role model?

"You look lost in thought."

Sabine's face was bright and open, with the happy look of a woman who knew down to her soul that she was loved by a good man. She was planning a wedding and setting up her life. Sabine juggled everything because her husband-to-be was off on a job interview.

Mackenzie would never be half the woman this lady was. "I was just thinking about the kind of person it takes to be supportive to a man who's gone so much."

Sabine did that nose-crinkling thing again. It made her look more like a young woman than a sophisticated lady. "I spent a lot of years being alone—I suppose I got used to it. Now that I have Doug, I know he's thinking about me as much as I'm thinking about him. Apart from that, you just keep busy with your life. When they get home, you make the most of the days you do have together. I'll say one thing for this life. It makes you take nothing for granted."

"I'm sure."

"You could do a lot worse than Aaron."

Mackenzie laughed and pushed back a wayward strand of hair that had escaped her bun. "I don't know if that kind of life is for me. Who knows what'll happen to me before all this is over? I don't see much point in false hope. Even if I thought Aaron was thinking about the future, I'm not. I can't."

"Doug's father told me that you have to let your heart answer the question. If it's what you both want, then God will make a way."

"I used to think that. But the reality is we have two completely different lives. Even if I did want a relationship, it looks impossible." Mackenzie sighed.

"It looked impossible to me, too." Sabine waved the fingers on her left hand. "And look where I'm at now."

That was nice for Sabine, being on the giddy-with-love side of things. It was easy to tout the blessings of a solid relationship and marriage when you already had it.

Being single was much harder.

Aaron growled. "Yes, I'd like to leave a message."

Why couldn't the Marshals Service office just say where Eric was? His brother hadn't answered his cell any of the times Aaron had called to tell him Mackenzie was fine. Something had to be going on if he wasn't sitting by his phone waiting to hear word on whether or not Aaron had gotten Mackenzie back.

Something serious.

At least that would explain why the office was giving him the runaround. But what was going on? Hopefully it meant that whoever leaked information had been found.

"Oh," another voice spoke in the background, and then the lady came back on the phone. "Marshal Harper, the marshal in charge of our office—"

"I know Steve is Eric's boss."

"Oh, well, he said if you let us know where you are, then we'll send a car to you and you can be here when he gets back. How does that sound? Eric shouldn't be long anyway. He just had something to see to."

A niggle of doubt scratched at Aaron's spine. "You can have Eric call me."

"Are you sure you don't want me to have us come to you?"

It was as if she was stalling him.

TWELVE

Aaron hung up the phone and ran a hand through his hair. If the marshals wanted to know his location, that couldn't mean anything good for Eric. He climbed back in the driver's seat but didn't shut the door.

"Something wrong?"

He didn't look back, instead dismissing Mackenzie's question with a jerk of one shoulder.

Out the corner of his eye, Sabine glanced between them. But she would have to deal with not knowing why he was being like this. He wasn't going to embarrass Mackenzie by explaining that he hadn't been about to kiss her. Even if—for just a moment—he'd really wanted to.

She was a good woman with a big heart; she just wasn't the kind who would put up with someone like him. Eventually he would disappoint her, and then there would be pain and heartbreak.

But that didn't mean he needed to be a jerk. "I'm worried about Eric. And I don't want to stick around here so those mercenaries can find us again. We need to be more careful." He turned back. There was hurt in her eyes. "In fact, give me your phone."

Mackenzie blinked. "My phone?"

"Yes. We don't need anyone tracking us." He shook his

own cell in front of her so she'd know that was what he meant. "So we're going to get rid of them."

"I don't have a phone."

Aaron exhaled. "Seriously? Everyone has a phone." Why was she being so difficult?

Sabine shifted in her seat. "She really doesn't have a phone." She was frowning. Why? He wasn't Doug. Aaron was used to disappointing people. "At least tell us what you know, Aaron. What's going on?"

"I think the marshals were trying to find out where we are. They're probably tracking my phone."

He cracked open the back of his phone, took out the SIM card because he'd need it later when this was all over and tossed the phone out the car. It bounced on the concrete and broke into pieces. Aaron slammed the door shut and fired up the engine.

Now Eric wouldn't be able to get hold of him; Aaron had just officially severed all contact. If he was a praying man, he'd ask for protection for Eric and Mackenzie. He didn't deserve any consideration for himself, but Eric and Mackenzie were two of the best people he knew. If anyone should have peace and happiness, it was them.

Aaron pulled onto the road. Two black SUVs sped up the street behind them, along with three police cars. Their lights were flashing, but sirens were quiet. He held his breath until they turned into the complex he'd parked in, then pressed on the gas and sped away.

Aaron glanced at Sabine. She'd seen the team coming for them. She gave him a short shake of her head. He wasn't sure if it meant that she didn't want Mackenzie to worry, or that she was disappointed in him. His charge had been kidnapped earlier, but he wasn't sure he wanted to start keeping stuff from her. But how was he supposed to keep her safe when their pursuers were so close behind?

How much more of this could Mackenzie take before
she broke? She'd been pretty strong so far, and even given
how scared she'd been in the warehouse she'd still recovered quickly. But how long would it last?

"Uh-oh."

Aaron took a left and headed for the freeway. He
glanced at Sabine. "What?"

She hit a button on her smartphone and held it up.

A news reporter's voice spoke over a picture of Eric.
"Deputy U.S. Marshal Eric Hanning was arrested just a
short time ago. He is suspected of selling information that
put specific persons who are part of the witness protection
program in danger."

Aaron pulled over to the side of the road.

He grabbed the phone, aware Mackenzie had leaned
forward to watch over his shoulder.

"A source inside the Marshals Service office informed
us that Hanning has worked for the Marshals Service for
eight years, the past six serving as a WITSEC inspector.
And now he has allegedly betrayed the very people he was
supposed to be protecting."

Mackenzie gasped. "No one's supposed to know."

"Someone just threw Eric under the bus."

"Law enforcement is also looking for two other people, a man and a woman, in connection with Marshal
Hanning's arrest."

A picture of Aaron beside Mackenzie flashed on the
phone's screen.

"The identity of the woman is as yet unknown, but the
man is U.S. Army Sergeant Aaron Hanning. He is the
brother of the arrested marshal and is suspected of colluding with him in this leak of highly classified information. He is also suspected of kidnapping the unidentified
woman."

The news reporter flashed a smug smile of perfect white teeth. "If you see either of these people, there is a number on-screen to call and report their whereabouts. We will provide more information as it comes to us."

"We're being set up." Aaron wanted to throw the phone or punch something. Sabine grabbed it out of his hand, probably not wanting to spend a few hundred bucks on a new phone right before her wedding.

"They think you kidnapped me?" Aaron turned back in time to see Mackenzie shake her head, her face pale. "This is unreal. What on earth is going on, Aaron? How could they think Eric is the mole in the office? He would never do that...to either of us. It's just not possible."

"I know that. You know that." Aaron sighed. "Someone is setting him up."

Sabine gritted her teeth. "They probably planted the evidence to make it look as if he was the mole. Get everyone's focus off the real mole and on looking for Mackenzie instead."

"And destroy all our lives in the process."

Sabine said, "Which makes sense if the mole is now helping Carosa. Because if they think Mackenzie's in danger, the police will be looking for her, and the marshals who know who she is will be trying to contain the leak. That means Carosa has even more of a chance of someone finding her and revealing her location."

Aaron frowned at Sabine. "Okay, seriously? You're supposed to be planning a wedding."

"Not anymore." Sabine looked smug. As though she knew he needed her and they both knew the help of a former CIA agent would be invaluable.

He did, but that didn't mean Doug wouldn't skin him if he got her hurt. "Sabine—"

"I think she should help us."

Aaron opened his mouth to tell Mackenzie it didn't matter what she thought, because he was the one who was going to keep her safe. He sighed. She'd had a rough day as it was. "Sabine is not even supposed to be here. Doug's going to knock me flat when he finds out I let her hang around when we've been repeatedly in danger."

Mackenzie pressed her lips together and nodded. "I don't want to run. I've done enough of that already."

"Carosa is going to be that much closer to finding you now."

"Then we have even less time than we did before to help Eric. And it's all the more important now."

"It's risky." But Aaron liked that she would put herself on the line for his brother. It was irrational, but emotions had never made sense to him.

She lifted her chin. "I can handle it. Can you?"

"Okay, we go after Eric's partner first. It's a good place to start. We'll snoop around and see if we can get something that will point to him as the mole so we can get Eric cleared. If it's not Schweitzer, we'll move on to the next guy, and the next. I'm not stopping. Eric will need all the help he can get." Aaron pinched the bridge of his nose. "He's pretty much done now that the reporter told everyone he works for WITSEC, but who knows? If we can get Eric out from under suspicion, maybe he can salvage his career."

Sabine's eyes were on him. "I'll give you all the info I have on the people he works with."

"And then you'll get lost."

She huffed. "Fine. But I'm calling Doug. If you get in even one sliver of trouble, he'll be expecting a call."

"Sabine—"

"You know he's going to be mad that you didn't call him in the first place."

Aaron figured that was probably about right. He started up the engine again. "Okay, let's get on with this."

Mackenzie could hardly believe what had happened. As familiar streets rolled by, she tried to assimilate the fact that Eric had been arrested, Aaron was suspected of kidnapping her and she was supposed to be the unwitting victim in all this.

Everyone would be looking for them. Carosa would find her even faster now, aided by ordinary people who called the hotline, thinking they were helping her. Did that reporter have any clue what she'd done? Apart from ruining Eric's career as a WITSEC inspector, provided he could get clear of whatever charges were against him and didn't end up in jail, the reporter had smeared the reputation of both brothers.

It was only a matter of time before someone who'd known her personally years ago—an old fan or acquaintance—saw the newscast and recognized her as Lani, and the fact that she used to be a pop star was made public.

Her heart broke for what Eric must be going through. She really liked him. Not romantically, but he seemed like such a caring guy.

A tear rolled down her face, and she wiped it away. Aaron glanced back at her and frowned. "You okay?"

"I'm just worried about Eric."

Sabine was talking on her cell phone, filling Doug in on what had happened. It seemed as though they had the kind of close relationship where they told each other everything. Mackenzie didn't even know how to be that vulnerable with someone. It would have to come with a whole lot of love and trust.

She wanted that with Aaron. Despite the fact that it would likely never happen, she couldn't help the jump of hope in her heart. Someday he might turn that intense devotion he felt for his family and friends toward someone else.

"I know that." Sabine sighed. "I know—"

She sighed and held out the phone to Aaron. "He wants to talk to you."

Aaron nodded. "Put it on speaker."

Sabine motioned toward Mackenzie. "Are you sure?"

"Just put it on speaker."

Mackenzie had too much buzzing around her head. She couldn't get mad that there might be things they wanted to keep from her. The three of them were close; it was obvious to anyone watching that Aaron had a huge amount of respect for his friend, which now extended to Sabine.

Aaron raised his voice. "Hey, man, what's up?"

"What's up?" The voice through the phone was low and tough, and crackled a bit. "You bring my fiancée along for the ride when you have mercenaries and cops after you? Are you crazy?"

"I didn't know the cops would be there."

"Sabine can't show up on anyone's radar. Ever. You know that."

Mackenzie studied the two of them in the front seats. Sabine held out the phone, her cheeks an endearing shade of pink as she said, "I kept a low profile. This isn't Aaron's fault."

Aaron sighed. "Mackenzie was kidnapped and Eric couldn't get away. There was no one else, and it turned out Sabine was on the case already."

"Yeah, she and I already talked about that. Maybe you guys should start a business, make all the car chases and gunfights official. I'll be your secretary."

Aaron snorted. Mackenzie couldn't imagine what a guy

with a voice this gruff would look like making coffee and typing up invoices.

"Were you just bored, was that it, Aaron? Looking for another thrill since you're on medical leave?"

Sabine sighed. "Doug—"

"Listen—" Aaron hit the turn signal so hard Mackenzie thought it might break. "Sabine saved Mackenzie's life. We needed help. More now, since Eric's been arrested. Mackenzie and I are going after the leak."

There was a big sigh over the line. "Sabine, stay in Phoenix. My flight leaves in an hour, so I'll be there tonight. I'll call my lawyer, too. We'll do everything we can for Eric. Aaron, just keep Mackenzie safe, and we'll talk later, okay?"

"Nothing like having cops on your tail to keep the mercenaries at bay."

Doug laughed. "No doubt, brother. Now drop my fiancée off."

The line went dead.

"I'm really sorry." Except it sounded as if Sabine was laughing.

Aaron smiled at Sabine. "He was like that before you. He's just worried, that's all."

Mackenzie watched Sabine smirk. "What is with this new and improved Aaron, who's all understanding and compassionate? I don't get it. Where'd you go? Where's the smooth-talking designer-clothes-wearing guy who used to be so shallow?"

"Ouch, Sabine."

"I know it was bad. I know—well, I'd need longer than this to check the pulse of how you're doing and where you're at, but I think maybe this time off might have done you good."

"Seriously?" His brow had crinkled and he didn't look

into fighting for his brother. She could see it in his eyes, in the way he held back, protecting himself. If the wound was too fresh, it explained why he hadn't told her.

Mackenzie got out when Sabine did and gave her a hug. Sabine squeezed her as though they were long-lost friends, and Mackenzie prayed that when this was over they could become that.

"Take care of him."

Mackenzie pulled back. Sabine was serious. "He needs taking care of?"

"More than he knows or would be willing to admit, ever. But he needs someone like you, Mackenzie. Someone who will see past the wet, angry kitty to the scarred heart underneath that wants to be loved. Just watch out for the claws."

Mackenzie didn't know whether to laugh or get mad at her description of Aaron. "I'm not sure that's exactly how it is…but okay."

Sabine laughed and hugged her again. "Trust me. You're exactly what he needs."

"I don't know about that."

"After what he's been through, you're perfect. Like fresh air."

Mackenzie wasn't completely convinced, but she was willing to trust this woman.

Aaron's door opened. Mackenzie looked back in time to see him scowl at them over the roof of the car. "If you're done having girl bonding time, can we go? There are people trying to kill us."

As if she could forget.

"'Bye, Sabine."

"Take care."

Mackenzie climbed in the front seat and buckled up. "So where to?"

Aaron huffed out a breath. "Let's just get on this. We'll start with Eric's partner."

Mackenzie wanted to ask how his shoulder was, since he had his hand in his lap and wasn't using it to drive. Did it hurt? But she kept her mouth shut, figuring the timing wasn't right to start her campaign to tame the angry kitty.

The corners of her mouth curled up. Aaron looked at her and did a double take. "What's funny?"

"I'll tell you later. But first, answer me this. Why Eric's partner that he mentioned?"

Aaron shrugged what she now knew was his good shoulder. "Eric seemed to think there was something there worth looking into. So until Sabine sends me all the info on the people he works with, it's a place to start, at least. And it's better than sitting here while Eric's in jail."

THIRTEEN

Mackenzie shifted in her seat beside him. They were parked outside a modest adobe house in the suburb of Scottsdale. The sun beat down on the hood of the car; just another day in Arizona. Her eyes were on the house, same as his.

He frowned at the back of her head. "Are you sure you want to do this today? You did get kidnapped this morning."

"I said I did. I wasn't lying. We have to help Eric."

Aaron rolled his eyes. He was exhausted, and his shoulder hurt something fierce. Rest would strengthen them both for the fight ahead. But no, Mackenzie didn't want to take a break. It bothered him, but why not admit to himself they had something in common, at least?

Why couldn't she see that he wanted to help Eric just as much as her? More, since Eric was *his* brother.

They were all tied up in this now. Sooner or later he was going to be arrested for kidnapping Mackenzie, and Eric would go to jail. But still, he was trying to be gracious. This wasn't her fight. She needed to concentrate on Carosa's threat to her life and let Aaron, Doug and Sabine help Eric.

"I just don't know why we can't leave it until tomorrow. It won't hurt anything to wait." She really did look as though she wanted to take a nap, and his shoulder was screaming with fire from having his arms restrained. Hers had to hurt, also.

"It'll hurt if more people's lives are ruined."

She rubbed at the marks on her wrists from the ties the mercenaries had used on her. His were the same, so when Aaron reached over and grabbed her hand, they matched. Her fingers were warm, her skin softer than anything he'd felt before. "Don't rub. You need to let it heal."

He should have bought some cream for her wrists, or a bandage, when he was picking up a prepay phone. Why didn't he do that? He sighed. He could be a real jerk sometimes.

"Are you okay?" Aaron studied her, but she didn't look at him. She just kept her eyes on the house they were watching. "My brother is innocent. Eric's record will speak for him and we'll help any way we can. You don't have to take on his cause, Mackenzie. You have enough to deal with."

He didn't want to leave his brother hanging, but sitting here with her, Aaron had to fight the urge to buy two plane tickets and get her out of there. Run. Never look back. It wouldn't solve either of their problems, but it sounded good anyway.

Mackenzie never answered. She just pulled up the email on Aaron's brand-new unregistered phone and read aloud, "1485 North Harrell is the home of Arnold Schweitzer, U.S. Marshal for the past fifteen years. Forty-seven years old. He's married, wife's name is Marcy and the kids are Helen, who's twelve, and Amy, nine. Now, tell me why we're sitting on the street four doors down from Mr. Schweitzer's house."

"It's called a stakeout."

"Okay…"

"You've never watched a cop show?"

She looked over at him. "I don't have a TV."

"Seriously?"

"Not everyone sits glued to a screen for hours on end. I do it enough at work with the computer. It's the last thing I want when I'm home."

"So you just sit around until bedtime?"

Mackenzie rolled her eyes. "No, I read. I had a five-thousand-piece puzzle that I was working on, but it was taking me a while because most nights I work late at the center."

Aaron pulled the phone over so he could see the file. He scanned down the page. "Eric didn't have anything he could pinpoint without an unsubstantiated illegal search into the life of a man he's supposed to trust. Sabine looked into his financial records, and there's nothing fishy, but at this point Eric's instinct is the best we've got."

"So…what are we doing now?"

Aaron glanced up at the roof of the car and sighed. "We're observing. Rule one of investigation is gathering information. The second is what we're doing right now. Looking for details to add to what we know."

"You mean like how the school bus came by and neither of the girls got off?"

"What?"

Mackenzie motioned to the house. "Why don't we go ask the neighbors why Marcy might be gone when her car is in the driveway, and why the girls didn't come home from school?"

"Fine." Aaron sighed. "You stay put, and I'll go talk to the neighbors."

"But if we split up, then we can cover twice as many houses."

"Which we're not going to do, because you need to rest. There's no point in overdoing it and not having time to regroup and get your strength back."

She looked over at him, her eyes narrowed. "Sounds like that's coming from experience."

Aaron shrugged. "I've been a soldier for a long time."

"So you've been injured?"

"Mostly fractures to fingers, toes, stuff like that. Busted ribs, concussions." He smoothed out a crease in his jeans. "Some injuries that were…worse."

"Like you were shot? Is that what happened to your shoulder?"

He zeroed in on the tone in her voice. "Why are you so fired up to talk about this? It's not fun. I'd think you would want to discuss anything else in the world than guns and war."

Hurt flashed on her face. "I was just making conversation."

Aaron sighed. "Let's go talk to the neighbors."

It didn't bode well how easily he was giving in to her just for the sake of avoiding *that* conversation. He badly needed to shore up his conviction and not let the pain in her eyes get to him. But it was tough. He had to remember this was about Eric, and Mackenzie was just a by-product. *Yeah, right.* Her death would be collateral damage, and he was trained to avoid that. That was why he was here. Doug and Sabine were perfectly capable of helping Eric clear his name.

By the time he got around to her door she'd already climbed out, and they walked together across the street. The neighbor's house was sun-bleached yellow with vinyl siding and a lawn of brown grass between the front door and the street. Blinds in the front window were pulled back, showing a wide-screen TV tuned to kids cartoons.

Aaron rang the bell and pandemonium erupted in the form of kids screaming and crying at the prospect of visitors. A woman answered the door with a stain on her T-shirt, her hair in a ponytail and no makeup. She squinted at the bright light outside. "Help you?"

"Is there anything you can tell us about the Schweitzers next door?"

The woman's eyes darkened. "Who wants to know? You guys cops or what? I'm not answering no questions to cops. I know my rights."

Mackenzie nudged him aside and got between Aaron and the woman. "It's nothing like that. We're friends of Marcy. We were supposed to visit with her today, but we must have missed her and Helen and Amy."

The woman corralled a toddler boy trying to crawl out the door between her feet. She looked back at Aaron and Mackenzie and sighed. "Helen and Amy come by after school most days to help me with the kids, unless they have soccer or whatnot. A week ago she texts me. Going to her sister's, she says. Family emergency or some such. And what am I supposed to do? I've got a business to run. Who's going to help me, huh?"

"We must have been mistaken, then, got our wires crossed or something. Thank you for your time." Aaron backed up, taking Mackenzie with him by her elbow.

Mackenzie waved at a couple of the kids. "Sorry to bother you."

When they reached the street, Mackenzie pulled her elbow out of his grip. Aaron snagged her hand with his, his mouth opening to say something, but when the warmth of her fingers folded around his, all thoughts left his head. This wasn't good. There weren't supposed to be any feelings between them. Aaron dropped her hand and ignored the glance she shot him. "Okay, so that was a pretty good idea. Now we know the wife and daughters went to her sister's, if we can believe it. We need to check the story and focus our attention on old Arnold."

She nodded and they climbed in the car.

Aaron pulled around the first corner and parked out of sight of Schweitzer's house. "Stay here."

Her eyes went wide. "Where are you going?"

"I'll be back in five minutes."

"What if you're not?"

He looked her in the eye. "I will be."

"Aaron—"

He shut the car door. Who knew how long it would be before the neighbor saw the news and called the police to report their whereabouts? If he needed to check out Schweitzer's house, he had to do it fast.

Mackenzie cranked the air-conditioning to max and slouched down in the seat so no one noticed her. Aaron had disappeared between two houses. A couple of doors up from the car an older teenage boy mowed a lawn, his shirt ringed with sweat. Across the street, two preteen girls lay out on their front lawn on deck chairs watching the show. Life was going on as normal. A car drove by, a low-to-the-ground model with a long hood.

Mackenzie sucked in a breath and squeezed her eyes shut. The sound of the engine diminished as it got farther away. It wasn't rational to be scared of every little thing just because there were a lot people looking for them. She couldn't live her life in fear. Not anymore. Wasn't there something in the Bible about that? Not being anxious or something.

The numbers on the dash clock clicked five minutes, and she watched for Aaron's return. Alone, Mackenzie could admit that attraction had stirred. She wanted to get to know him better and see where it could lead. But while they had been close in proximity, him comforting her when she needed it, he still seemed so far away and removed from her.

Mackenzie had plenty of secrets of her own, but for the right man she was more than willing to open up. Could Aaron say the same? She wasn't sure.

At the six-minute mark, she had grabbed the door handle, ready to go after him, when another car, high-end and not like she would have thought a government employee would drive, pulled around the corner. Mackenzie lifted up an inch and checked out the driver. It was the same guy whose picture had been on the email: Schweitzer.

She slid back down in the seat.

There was no way to warn Aaron that Schweitzer was coming. If he found Aaron in his house, he would surely shoot him, especially when he saw who it was. Or he would arrest Aaron for kidnapping her, and then Mackenzie would be on her own.

She opened the door just as Aaron jogged around the corner.

"What are you doing?" He hissed, "Shut that door."

"Schweitzer came back. I thought he was going to kill you."

Aaron climbed in. "Buckle up. Now."

She waited until he buckled his seat belt and then said, "What took you so long? I was worried. I really thought he was going to find you in there and kill you."

"Seriously?" He pulled away from the curb. "I wouldn't let that happen. I wouldn't leave you on your own."

"I was worried about you."

"Because you'd get left alone."

"I would have been fine." *Hopefully.* Mackenzie crossed her arms. "Am I not allowed to worry about you?"

"Don't know why you would. Most people wouldn't think I was worth it."

Except for Doug and Sabine, who seemed to have a profound devotion to this man. That alone seemed to indicate there was something special about him, despite what he seemed to think. "Schweitzer didn't find you?"

"I was just having a look around. Heard his car pull in, headed out the gate in the backyard. Everything's fine, Mackenzie."

That wasn't true. But it was nice of him to say it. As though if it wasn't then she could trust him to make it that way.

"Please tell me you didn't actually break into that house."

"Rest assured, no laws were broken. I just looked in the back windows."

Had she really been worried he might have killed Schweitzer? Sometimes Aaron acted all no-nonsense soldier and other times he came across like a smooth old West cowboy. The first, she was recognizing, was his work mode. She wondered if the other was the real him. It seemed so…practiced. Was he purposely trying to be charming?

"So what did you do in there?"

He studied the road as he drove, giving plenty of attention to his rearview mirror. Was he looking to see if someone was following them? Mackenzie should probably learn how to do that. It might come in handy…what with there being a man trying to kill her and all.

He gave her a double take. "You okay?"

Mackenzie turned and nodded to the window. "Sure."

"That wasn't breaking and entering, what I did back there. I only break into criminals' houses when I'm asked, and there's nothing concrete to suggest this guy isn't legit. At least, not yet."

She looked at him. "You break into criminals' houses?"

He was smiling, but he didn't look happy. "For my job. The one I do far from here, in hot-as-a-sauna countries where innocent people have no voice and no one to fight for them."

"Wow." It just came out. Mackenzie wasn't sure why she said it, only that it was an honest response from her heart. "Is that why you do it?"

"Pays the bills."

"So you don't want anyone to know you have a heart, or that your job involves some kind of higher purpose? You'd rather brush off the notion that you have an ingrained sense of honor." Mackenzie looked away again.

When Aaron spoke, his voice was flat. "We can't all have some grand calling like you, helping turn around at-risk kids. Not everyone feels a sense of destiny at their jobs. For most people, work is just work. You go, you suffer through it and then you go home and try to escape the fact that you have to do it again tomorrow."

Mackenzie frowned. Was that really what he thought of the world, that life was drudgery? "I happen to think it's a big deal that you are a soldier, putting your life at risk for the cause of freedom. It is honorable. Something to be proud of."

He pulled the car to the side of the road and looked away, out the side window. When he spoke, his voice was low. "You're wrong."

FOURTEEN

"Aaron—"

His head whipped around, his eyes desolate. What she'd been about to say dissipated and she cleared her throat. She couldn't ask him what he meant. From the look on his face, it would be a while before she could go there. "At least tell me if you learned anything, looking around at the Schweitzers'."

He sighed. "Kitchen sink is full. Counters looked crowded with cereal boxes and empty jars of peanut butter, so the neighbor was probably right about the wife being gone. The only other window I could see in was the patio, just a view of the hall. But the shih tzu wanted out pretty badly."

"They have a puppy?"

"A very unhappy one. Nearly yapped my ear off when it saw me over the fence."

Mackenzie sighed. "So all we have is a bunch of dirty dishes and a dog?"

"No signs of a struggle that I saw, no broken windows. The wife is most likely fine, at her sister's with the kids—"

"In the middle of the school semester. Without taking the car."

"Even so, it's the most likely conclusion." He started

up the car. "We can follow Schweitzer and see where he goes from here. See if it leads us—"

The fancy car went by them again, this time in the other direction.

"That's him."

Aaron pulled out into traffic, a ways back from Schweitzer's car.

Mackenzie chewed her lip. Somewhere along the way their conversation had taken a turn for the worse. Aaron was no longer deflecting her with lighthearted banter. He had shut down completely into some kind of business-only mode. So why did that make her want to dig deeper and draw him out of his shell?

Aaron kept a solid distance, but his eyes were on Schweitzer's taillights. If this was a mission, he would have someone tracking Schweitzer's phone and giving him the location so he could hang back out of sight. There would be more than one car following the target, and all of this would have been coordinated ahead of time.

As it was, all he had was a sullen Mackenzie and his training, which hadn't amounted to much when everything that could've gone wrong had. She wanted him to open up and tell her about it, but he just didn't want to see the look on her face when she found out he was a complete failure—that because of him, a friend of his, who was a good man and a good soldier, was now blind.

Aaron sighed. He should probably just quit the army as soon as he could. That would be better than living with the shame of what he'd done to the team. He could start his own business, though that would probably take more money than he had. Doug's idea of a partnership sounded pretty good, not that Doug would be the secretary. Sabine wouldn't put up with that either, so they would probably have to hire someone to run the office.

He could maybe see what Mackenzie thought about it. She seemed to have set up a new life pretty well and found something that made her happy. How did she know what that was?

Schweitzer drove into downtown, which was busy with cars on this hot summer evening. People moved everywhere, some of them probably on the lookout to save the "unnamed woman" from the big bad abductor. Schweitzer turned left well before they reached the Downtown Performing Arts Center. Mackenzie's disappointment was plain, but it was for the best. She needed to stay clear of places where people would recognize her.

They followed Schweitzer to a parking garage and wound around the ramp to the top floor where he'd parked. Aaron pulled into a space across the aisle, several cars down from Schweitzer. Aaron turned their vehicle around and backed in so they could see Schweitzer and get out fast if need be.

Aaron wanted to call someone, to let people who could help them know what they were doing. He needed his team, but he and Mackenzie were all alone. How long would it take before his heart realized his team was never going to accept him back?

Schweitzer headed for the doors, the entrance to a chain hotel above the garage. But he didn't push the button. He checked his gold watch and just waited.

Mackenzie glanced at him. "Should we get out and follow him?"

"Let's just hang here and see who he's waiting for."

A car passed them, a red soft-top Mustang he'd seen before. The woman driving the car was the same woman he'd seen at the center. What was her name?

Mackenzie sucked in a breath. "Eva."

She grabbed the door handle. Aaron put his hand on her arm. "Don't. You need to stay here."

Mackenzie stared at the scene in front of her as Eva parked and sashayed to the elevator, hitting the button to lock her car over her shoulder. She strode right to Schweitzer, and then there was no doubt. Mackenzie couldn't pass it off as coincidental when Eva flung herself into the marshal's arms and they kissed…for long enough that Mackenzie had to look away.

But if Schweitzer was dirty, that meant Eva was involved in more than just an illicit relationship with a married man. She was involved with Carosa, too. How was that possible?

Aaron started the car and pulled out of the space, not saying anything while her heart tore open. In all the years since she'd had an actual real friend, she had never expected that the first person she would actually want to be friends with would betray her like this.

As they drove away, a gunshot echoed through the garage.

Mackenzie squealed and looked out the rear window. Schweitzer lay on the ground. Eva was standing over him with a gun in her hand, pointed at his chest.

"She killed him. Eva killed him."

Aaron didn't say anything; he just kept driving, as if the dissonant fragments of Mackenzie's life hadn't just crumbled all over again.

"Why would she kiss Schweitzer and then kill him?" Mackenzie sucked in a breath, fighting against the tightness in her chest. "Why did she come to the center? I thought she loved the kids, but she's a killer, too. She betrayed me."

"I know." He pulled up to the exit and handed the guard five dollars while Mackenzie wrung her hands and tried to get her breathing under control.

"Why would she do that?"

Aaron pulled forward and slowed the car to a stop at the exit.

The windshield splintered, Aaron grunted and the car moved forward as if his foot had slipped off the brake. He gripped the steering wheel again, and they pulled out into traffic.

Mackenzie saw the red on his face. "You're bleeding." She gasped. "You've been shot!"

He drove, blinking even though blood now tracked down his cheek. It was running freely and he was squinting to see out the shattered windshield.

"You need a cloth or something."

"I need a car I can see out of." He pulled onto a side street but looked out the side window. "And a rifle so I can return the favor."

He winced, and Mackenzie dug around in the glove box but found no napkins. What kind of person didn't keep napkins in their glove box? She grabbed her backpack and found her shirt from yesterday. She balled it up and pressed it against his temple.

Aaron winced but kept driving. He reached up and took over with the cloth.

Mackenzie looked down at her hands.

There was blood on her.

Again.

Black spots peppered her vision. Mackenzie struggled to breathe. Aaron called her name, but she couldn't reply.

Aaron pressed the pedal to the floor and the car tore down the street. He wished he could take his frustration out on whoever had shot at them. Mackenzie was out of it, lost in whatever had made her eyes go distant. But he couldn't help her right now. If they hung around, they could get picked off by another shot from that sniper.

He kept one hand on the balled-up piece of cloth, pressing hard against his head. It wasn't more than a scratch, though it had been made by a sniper round.

The thing had barely grazed him, going as fast as it had, but the heat and the speed had been close enough to his head that it felt like being kissed by fire. Hopefully his free-flowing head wound would quit bleeding soon and wouldn't need stitches, because they didn't have time to stop off at the hospital.

They were running *again*. It wasn't in his makeup to turn tail and do anything other than fight his way out of a situation, and yet that seemed to be what he was doing with Mackenzie at every turn. He should be toe-to-toe with these mercenaries, making Mackenzie safe and clearing Eric's name, but he was driving away instead.

He slammed the heel of his palm against the steering wheel.

This whole situation had done nothing but go from bad to worse, and now Mackenzie's friend was involved. How could that be possible? There had to be a link between the Carosa family, Eric's partner at the Marshals Service office and Eva. Though evidently Schweitzer and Eva had been having an affair...at least up until the point she shot him.

Aaron had already found the on-ramp to the freeway going north. Without really thinking about it, he knew where he was taking her. There was nothing either of them could do for Eric. All Aaron needed was to make sure Mackenzie was safe, and there was nowhere better for that than the cabin.

Technically he wasn't supposed to be there, since it belonged to the team. He hadn't exactly left in good standing, and it grated that he couldn't go visit his teammate in the hospital. But hopefully when they found out about Mackenzie they'd forgive him for intruding on their private space.

Then again, Aaron's face had been all over the news. If his team had seen it, they probably thought he'd gone completely off the rails—from failure to abductor in just a week. How would he ever get his career back after this?

The cabin would give him and Mackenzie the space they needed to regroup instead of being forced to react to what was happening at every turn. They needed to get ahead of the curve so Aaron could turn all this in their favor for once. He'd always hated playing defense.

A low moan came from Mackenzie. Aaron reached over and squeezed her hand to try to alleviate the heavy feeling in his chest. "You okay?"

She drew in a shuddering breath. "Are *you* okay? I mean, your head and everything."

Aaron touched the skin around the wound. It had stopped bleeding finally. "It's just a graze. Head wounds bleed a lot."

"I'm sorry I freaked out." Her eyes were dark with something he couldn't see. "It was like a nightmare, but while I was still awake. I was right back in the hotel room with Carosa pointing his gun at me."

Aaron focused on the road again. "I'm sorry, Mackenzie."

Her face was turned to the side window, and her voice was low when she said, "It felt as though it happened all over again. My chest still hurts."

"You were shot?"

She nodded and pressed her fingers just below her collarbone on the left side, high enough that the damage had healed—because any lower and she'd be dead.

Aaron squeezed the fingers of the hand he still held in an effort to give comfort, as much for himself as for her.

Mackenzie was just a friend, if that. It certainly wasn't rational to think there was anything more between them. So why did he want to stand in front of her like a shield and protect her from everything in the world that might harm her?

He was no hero.

But considering what had already happened to her, there wasn't much Aaron could do to make it worse. Or better, really. And that made him feel useless all over again—knowing she'd already nearly died and spent half her life in hiding. He was torn between anger at his powerlessness and the overwhelming urge to hug her. There were no do-overs, but if he had the power to wipe it all away for her, he would have.

Eventually the mercenaries would catch up to them again. Which begged the question…how did they seem to know where Aaron and Mackenzie were at all times? First on the way to the restaurant, then the park, the hotel and now exiting the parking lot, they'd been found over and over again. It was a wonder they were both still alive.

Aaron found a rest stop and pulled off the highway to a far corner that wasn't lit by streetlight. The whole area was deserted except for a lone semi by the restrooms. "Give me your bag."

"Why? Are we leaving the car? How will we get anywhere on foot? There's nothing but desert here."

Aaron swiped the backpack from the floor by her feet and rummaged through it. "We're not walking. Those mercenaries seem to know where we are every time we turn around. We need to figure out how they are tracking us or we'll never get away."

Mackenzie grasped for the backpack. "Where's your bag? Are you going to give it to me so I can search through it as if *you're* a criminal?"

Aaron shuffled her things around. "That's not what I'm doing." His fingers found a rip in the lining at the bottom. Inside was a solid object. He pulled it out. "Thought you didn't have a cell phone."

"I don't." Mackenzie's eyes widened. "I've never seen that before."

"Really?"

He studied her. There was no reason to believe she would lead the mercenaries to them. It was more likely that the phone had been planted there. But he had to be sure. "Are you certain?"

"Some of the kids have phones like that. I've never used one. I didn't buy that." Was this really happening? "This is unreal."

"Actually, it's very real. This phone is on, which means someone is tracking us. They've been tracking us this whole time."

"Get rid of it then! Throw it out the window, or, I know! Run over it with the tire!"

Those weren't bad ideas, but Aaron had more questions. "Could Eva have put this in your bag?"

"She didn't know about my go bag. It was in my hall closet at home. It's just for emergencies, and since Eric's the one who told me to have a bag like this, he brought it to me."

"Was she at your house any time when you were in a different room, when she could have put it in your bag?"

"To plant a cell phone on me? That would mean she knew...about Carosa. About everything."

Aaron's voice was hard. "She was having an affair with Schweitzer. She probably *did* know everything."

Mackenzie could barely look at Aaron. Shame filled her in a hot rush that was all too familiar. "I just don't know how she could have fooled me. Do you think she's behind all this?"

"I don't know, Mackenzie. But we'll figure it out."

"Why would she do this to me?" She sighed. "Do we have to follow her now? Because I don't know if I can stomach that."

Mackenzie didn't ever want to see Eva again.

"We're not following her. We need time to rest and space to regroup, and we're not going to get that on the lam with a bunch of mercenaries following us." He yanked the door handle and got out for a second, crouching at the front tire. "Your suggestion on how to deal with the phone wasn't bad."

He got back in, gunned the engine and drove over the phone. Then he brought his foot up over the dash and kicked out the shattered front windshield.

FIFTEEN

Hours later Aaron drove down the highway with the wind blowing in his face. There had been a hole in the middle of the glass where the bullet had punched through the windshield.

Mackenzie had crawled into the backseat to sleep. She hadn't wanted him to drive alone, but the exhaustion on her face was clear. That was why he'd suggested she get some rest. There wasn't much more of this she could take.

The unsettled feeling in Aaron's stomach dissipated as, for the first time in a long time, he prayed for Eric, and for Doug, who was by now gathering information to prove Eric's innocence. Because he *was* innocent. Everything about Eric was innocent, it always had been.

Aaron could admit—to himself, at least—that sometimes prayer was the only option to offer a shred of hope. And right now, that was all they had left. Hope. For the first time Aaron was willing to consider the possibility that his foster mom was right, that Doug and Eric were right. Maybe it was worth it to put his faith in God.

Especially when he had nothing else left.

The career Aaron had spent years building, brick by brick, had come crumbling down until he was left with nothing but failure. Since he'd signed up for the military just out of high school, he'd always known who he was and where he was headed. Now the road was shrouded in mist, and there was nothing to light the way.

Just before five o'clock in the morning, the new phone he'd bought at a superstore buzzed. It had been a tough decision, but staying out of contact completely meant not knowing what was happening with Eric. Though having to get a car charger and a Bluetooth had cut into his cash reserves significantly. But he wasn't going to stop driving, not even to take a call.

He tapped the button on his Bluetooth. "Yeah."

"Where are you?" Doug's voice was groggy.

"On the highway."

"Are you going where I think you're going?"

There was a shuffle in the backseat. Mackenzie had awoken, even though he'd been talking quietly. "You know it's the only place, the safest place to regroup."

"Did you figure out how they've been tracking you?"

Aaron blew out a breath. "Yeah, after one of their snipers winged my temple."

"You okay?" Doug's voice cleared of all trace of fatigue.

"Doesn't even need stitches." Not that Aaron had checked—he just assumed by the fact that it'd finally stopped bleeding. At the last rest area he'd found a first-aid kit in the trunk and stuck on a bandage while Mackenzie slept.

He told Doug about Schweitzer and Eva.

Doug growled. "They found Schweitzer's body. You're saying Eva shot him?"

He gripped the steering wheel with one hand and saw the turnoff for the access road. Slowing the car, Aaron removed his foot from the brake, flipped off the headlights and took the turn. To anyone following, their car would have simply disappeared.

"Looked like some kind of tiff. They were clearly having an affair, but he did something to make her mad or else she was done using him."

"I'm going to grab Sabine from her hotel room and we'll head to Schweitzer's house now, and then the Marshals Service office. We'll find out what's going on. Hopefully there's something there that will get Eric in the clear." Doug paused a beat. "You guys stay safe, yeah?"

"Got it." Aaron tossed the Bluetooth in the cup holder, slowed to a crawl and flipped the headlights back on to light the way up the mountain to the cabin.

"Is everything okay?" Mackenzie asked.

He nodded. "Doug and Sabine are on the case." And he hoped all that desperate prayer would help. They definitely needed it.

"But no one is going to believe us that Eva killed Schweitzer. They think we broke the law, too, don't they? That we're in league with Eric, you kidnapped me and no doubt I probably did something illegal, too."

"We don't need them to believe us, Mackenzie. The evidence will speak for itself. There were probably security cameras in the parking garage. And if Eva does manage to get away with it, then Doug and Sabine will find proof she's involved with Carosa. There has to be something linking them more than Schweitzer, if his relationship with Eva is what made him betray the marshals. Maybe she works for Carosa or owes him money or something. Who knows until we find out for sure?"

She brushed back hair from her face. There was an endearing crease on her cheek from where her head had rested on her sweater. "So where are we?"

Aaron steered around the switchbacks up the mountain. "It's a hunting cabin the team uses. No one knows about it except us, and its ownership is buried so deep no one would ever be able to trace it back to us. It's a little rough, but we'll be safe here."

After their slow ascent up the dirt track to the top of the mountain, Mackenzie followed Aaron into the rough cabin. Apparently their definitions were different, because she might have been a millionaire pop star in her former life, but she was in no way overreacting. This place wasn't fit for a family of mice.

She took a deep breath and swallowed what she was going to say. Aaron had chosen this place for them to be safe, and it wouldn't help them if she put up a fuss now. Unless he'd lured her there to kill her, but she didn't think that was likely. It did pay to be cautious, though.

"Just needs a little sprucing up and it'll be fine."

Mackenzie turned to him, able to feel the way her face had morphed to incredulity.

Aaron burst out laughing. "Okay, so it'll keep the wind and rain out. The rest we can fix with a wet rag and a broom."

"Right." Mackenzie couldn't help but smile at the mental image of Aaron wearing rubber gloves with a bandanna tied around his head.

There was a table and four rickety chairs, an outdated kitchen with grime in the sink, but a stocked cupboard of cleaning supplies that looked as if they'd never been used. The bathroom walls were a weird shade of green, and the bedroom had two twin beds with bare mattresses.

The back door led out to a clearing. Mackenzie watched the trees sway in the breeze, closed her eyes and breathed in fresh air, feeling it rush through the cabin from front to back to air out the structure.

There was a rustling, and she opened her eyes. A deer stepped out of the trees and sniffed at the ground. Here in the middle of nowhere. What state were they in? Wherever it was, they were a world away from Carosa and the responsibilities she'd heaped on her own shoulders. That hardly seemed to matter now, here, where the world rustled instead of buzzing and shouting.

A boot clicked on the wood of the deck. Mackenzie spun around and Aaron stilled, holding a man-size overcoat out in front of him. "Just me. I thought you might be cold."

Mackenzie let him wrap the massive coat around her shoulders. "Thank you." She studied his face. "How's your head?"

Aaron shrugged.

"Does anything bother you?"

His lips twitched. "Like my brother being in federal custody while I can't do a single thing about it, or like a Colombian drug lord on our tail every time we turn around?"

"I can't believe that reporter thinks Eric had anything to do with this." She sighed. "It feels as though, if it wasn't for me, he wouldn't have been targeted."

"This isn't your fault, Mackenzie. Eric knows what he's doing and he's not alone."

He looked so dejected.

"What happened on your mission?" Mackenzie gasped. She'd said it before the thought even registered.

Why had she pushed him that way? Things were nice and now she'd ruined it. "I'm sorry. That was uncalled for. You don't have to tell me something so personal."

As much as she might want him to open up, it couldn't be because she had pushed. It had to be because he wanted to share. She turned to go back inside, and he snagged her elbow.

"Stay. Just for a minute."

Mackenzie nodded.

Aaron looked out at the clearing. The deer had moved

on, leaving only whispering branches and the chill of morning. "There's a lot I can't tell you because it's classified. But it was a bad plan, drawn up by someone who didn't seem to care either way that our lives and the lives of civilians who lived around the compound would be at risk. We were in the middle of a firefight, but taking the designated route out would have resulted in too many casualties. Civilians. I just couldn't do it. So I ordered my team to hold tight. It was my decision. It took longer, but we got out. And the cost was still high."

Mackenzie stepped closer but didn't dare touch him when his body was coiled this tight.

Aaron's eyes flickered and darkened. "At the end of the day, the results of the mission are on me. We did what we were sent in there to do, but one of my teammates was blinded in the fight."

He turned to her then. "I have to live with that. It will color my whole career, but I have to face what happened. I did what I thought was right, but then I always knew I wasn't a hero."

At the sound of a car, Aaron grabbed the loaded rifle he'd stashed on top of the bookcase and strode out the front door. He needed Mackenzie to realize he wasn't the kind of guy a girl like her should fall for.

Mackenzie probably wanted to run now that she knew the whole sordid tale of his failure. It was for the best, even if he did feel like mourning the loss of what might have been.

He'd heard the sound of an engine approaching before he could finish his speech, and sure enough, a black-and-white car was parked out front. It had a light bar on top and the word *sheriff* emblazoned on the side. Aaron held the weapon loosely, angled to the ground so he could bring it up and be firing a round in seconds.

He'd been expecting this visit, but a person could never be too careful.

The tall, wiry man folded himself out of the vehicle. His lean body was exactly the same as it had been when he and Aaron had served together. Aaron's old teammate walked over, his eyes narrowed. "Hey."

Aaron lifted his chin. "Slow morning?"

The sheriff's lips twitched. "You tripped the sensors when you went inside. I drove by, saw the tire tracks in the road and wanted to make sure it was you. Figured you'd come here, what with needing to hide that girl you abducted and all." He lifted his chin. "So who is she?"

Aaron didn't answer. "The media didn't figure it out yet?"

The other man cracked a smile and shook his head. "You never did like sharing. Do I need my gun, too?"

Aaron walked back to the cabin and set the rifle down so it leaned against the wall beside the door. "Mackenzie, you wanna come out here?"

The door cracked an inch. Her eyes were wide and darted between him and the cop car. "Is it safe?"

Aaron nodded. "There's someone I want to introduce you to." Plus it would clear up the idea the media had that he'd been mistreating her, since Aaron was the one with the head wound.

She came out and stood behind him, so his body shielded her from the local lawman. The fact that she still had faith in him to protect her felt good. "Is he going to arrest us?"

Aaron took her hand and pulled her to where the other man stood. "Mackenzie Winters, this is Sheriff Jackson Tate."

"Nice to meet you, ma'am."

She nodded. "Uh…you, too."

They shook hands, but Mackenzie hadn't completely pushed off her nervousness. Aaron squeezed the hand he still held. "Jackson and I were on the same Delta Force team a few years back. We're old army buddies."

"He's not going to arrest us?"

The sheriff laughed. "I was never here. Except to give Aaron this." He strode back to the car and opened the passenger door to retrieve a taped brown box the size of a small TV.

Aaron studied the address labels. "We get mail now?"

"They sent it to me on the off chance you might stop by here during your, uh…convalescence." Jackson smirked.

"Mackenzie knows about that." Aaron tucked the box under his arm.

"Right. I was sorry to hear about Franklin."

"Not as sorry as I am."

SIXTEEN

"Anyway, I might be able to help y'all. If you need it." The sheriff glanced between them. "Keep an eye out. I can watch the cabin's perimeter when I'm not working, that kind of thing."

It was too risky. "We're good."

Mackenzie glanced at Aaron. "He's offering to help. And we've sure needed it so far. You have a bullet wound, and Eric's in jail. The sheriff is offering to help. I thought you guys worked in teams?"

"This isn't one of our missions, and Jackson has enough to worry about. If he gets tangled up in this it could mean he loses his job. It's a gray area for him to even be here in the first place. If anyone found out he knew we were here and didn't bring us in, he'd get in a whole heap of trouble."

The sheriff leaned forward. "For what it's worth, he's right. I knew he wouldn't let me help, but that doesn't mean I won't have my eyes and ears open while you're here, whether Aaron likes it or not."

"Jackson—" Aaron growled his friend's name.

But Jackson waved his hand. "Deal with it."

Aaron raised his eyebrows. The man was willing to risk his family? "How are the girls? How old is Lena now? Six? Seven?"

"Six."

Aaron put his free hand in his pocket and rocked back on his heels. "And Ellie, how's your wife these days?"

Jackson practically pouted. "She's pregnant."

"Congratulations, Jackson."

Point made.

Jackson sighed. "Fine I won't help. At all."

"It's just not worth risking them." The risk to himself wasn't worth mentioning. But then he didn't have a wife and a family.

Jackson's lips thinned. "Enjoy your package."

"Thank you. I will." But his hands shook when he took it. He turned and strode inside.

Mackenzie glanced at the front door of the cabin, which, surprisingly, hadn't fallen off its hinges with the force of Aaron's mood. "Is he mad at you?"

The sheriff's face creased in a way that let her know he smiled often. "He doesn't want me putting my family at risk. It's okay, Mackenzie."

"I get the feeling he only cares about his brother, and maybe his friends. He and I hardly know each other."

"The Aaron Hanning I know never leaves anything unfinished. It's a pain when you have to cut and run because that's what you were ordered to do, or when the situation turns and everything goes sour. There are few things Aaron despises more than not meeting the expectations he set for himself."

Mackenzie blew out a breath. The more she got to know Aaron, the more the layers peeled back. She'd only scratched the surface. "Maybe we shouldn't be talking about this. He might not want to share that stuff with me."

"One more thing and I'll get out of your hair."

Mackenzie smiled. "What's that?"

He reached back and Mackenzie wondered for a minute if he was going to pull a gun on her. She must have reacted, because his eyes widened as he pulled out his business card. "Just in case."

She looked down at multiple phone numbers and an email address for Sheriff Jackson Tate. "Thank you."

"Call if you need anything."

Mackenzie watched him drive away and ached to leave this place, to go somewhere—anywhere—simply for the sake of being free of Carosa. But that wouldn't work. He would hunt her until one of them was dead.

It might be little more than a dream, to think about being a free woman one day. Every single time was a struggle, but the more she practiced, the easier it would be to keep giving control of her life to God. But the reality was, she also had to let go of the past.

Until then, all she had was the dream of what could be. Even if she didn't believe it would ever come true.

Aaron looked out the window as his friend drove away. Good. Jackson really needed to get back down the mountain to his family. The longer he spent with Aaron and Mackenzie, the bigger the risk that he would be caught in the cross fire. Aaron had no intention of giving bad news to Jackson's wife and daughter. Not when it would be all his fault.

He already had enough on his conscience.

Aaron slumped onto the couch and ran a hand down his face just as the door shut.

"Does it hurt?" Mackenzie settled beside him. She touched the bandage on his temple, and he gritted his teeth to keep from swatting her hand away. "It looks better. Not that that's saying much."

The couch moved again, but he kept his eyes closed.

"So how come Jackson knew about this place when you said no one would find us here? I thought this was some kind of secret hideout for your team. How can it be if the local sheriff knows about you?"

"I told you, he was part of the team before."

"And he just decided to move here on a whim?"

Aaron shrugged. "It helped to have someone to look out for the place, and his wife wanted to get out of the city. They were in Los Angeles, and she was worried about little Lena."

There was a minute of silence, so he turned. She wanted to ask him something, so he waited.

"At least tell me what state we're in. Utah? Nevada?"

Aaron smiled. "It's not as though I blindfolded you."

"I was asleep. Same thing."

"We're in Colorado."

"Huh."

He motioned for her to continue, since she was apparently going to talk nonstop the whole time they were here. Aaron briefly wondered if there were any noise-canceling headphones in the cabin.

"It's just…I've been to Denver and all. So I've done the Colorado scene, but that was years ago. And I haven't even been out of Phoenix since I moved there. It's part of being in WITSEC. Not that you can't vacation, but I've been to nearly every major city there is, so it doesn't leave many options for traveling and meeting the requirements of witness protection so that I stay where people won't recognize me."

"You don't camp?"

"Uh…no." She shuddered hard enough it shook the couch.

"Fish?"

She shook her head.

"Surf?"

"I tried it once. I couldn't stand up. Like, at all. It was too wobbly, then I hit my head on the board and I thought I was going to throw up. It wasn't a good experience."

Right. Aaron studied her. "So you just work at the center now? Nothing else. No hobbies or anything?"

"Nope."

"What about before?"

"I was all about the music. And then suddenly I wasn't allowed to play anymore because someone might hear me sing and realize who I was. I risked it at the center, late at night. Enough years had passed, and people had pretty much forgotten about me."

She chuckled but without any humor. "Which makes me feel great. Sometimes it's enough to hear someone singing, but I get to the point I can't breathe if I don't play guitar. I need the music. Otherwise it's as if I can't…feel anything."

Aaron nodded, though he didn't really get it. There wasn't anything in his world that made him feel alive like that.

"So what was in your package?"

"Don't know. I didn't open it yet."

She glanced at the back of the cabin. "Do you want me to go in the bedroom?"

Aaron grabbed the box and pulled it across the table. "That's not necessary."

He hesitated with the flaps. The inside was packed with balled-up newspaper. Aaron dug it out and found a plastic container with half a dozen chocolate chip cookies in it. Below that was a game console wrapped in bubble wrap. A remote and a stack of games were with it. Car-racing games mostly, nothing that involved shooting bad guys, since they got enough of that in real life.

"This doesn't seem bad."

Aaron kept his eyes on the box and nodded. They'd told him not to visit Franklin in the hospital until he was asked. So why this, why now?

Mackenzie shifted forward on the couch. "They must not have thought it was so bad that the mission went wrong. Not if they sent you a care package."

Aaron pulled out the games and set them on the table. At the bottom of the box was a white envelope. He ripped down one end and dumped the contents into his palm.

The silver dollar was cold and sat heavy in his hand.

"Does that mean something?"

Aaron bit his lip.

"Aaron?"

"Yes—" He cleared his throat. "It means something."

He got up and went outside with the coin gripped in his fist. Wetness tracked down his face and he swiped it away. The screen door snapped back on its hinges and he turned away, hoping she wouldn't see the emotion on his face.

"There's a note."

He turned. Mackenzie held up a piece of paper. He took it from her and unfolded it.

Franklin told us.

"Your friend who was blinded? What did he tell them?" She backed up a step. "Sorry. You probably don't need me butting in. It's none of my business."

Aaron grabbed her hand and pulled her to him so their shoulders touched. "When it happened, they needed someone to blame for us getting in that situation. It's tough to think straight in the middle of a firefight. Your focus narrows, almost to a single point. Between the four of us we could cover the area surrounding us, but that meant they didn't see the shot that ricocheted and blinded Franklin. They were firing, covering us as we moved, and it was up to me to watch out for the man beside me.

"Franklin was injured and they needed somewhere to put their anger. Honestly, I was fine with it. Now I know they've blown through their ire and they're ready for me to come back."

"And you didn't tell them it wasn't your fault?"

She really thought that? "I'm the team leader, so it was on me. My responsibility. They were right to say what they said." Aaron squeezed her hand. If he was honest, he didn't ever want to let go. "They know I couldn't have changed the outcome. This is their apology for shutting me out, but not for blaming me. And that's okay."

"Cookies?"

He laughed. "Works for me."

"But you still feel responsible."

"I am responsible. Franklin will never be a soldier again. It was my first time being team leader and this happened."

Something clicked in his mind, and Aaron got why faith had come so easily to Eric. His brother also understood that his actions dictated the consequences he had to live with. But Eric seemed to have been able to give that up to God—to let Him wash away Eric's culpability.

Aaron had to live with the consequences of what had happened on the mission. So why should he seek forgiveness for something that was his fault in the first place? Where was the fairness in that?

"The coin means Franklin is on the mend. It means I can visit him in the hospital and there won't be any resentment."

"That's good."

"It is. Because they've been part of my life for years now. A family, a group of brothers. I'll need their support when I get back." He looked at Mackenzie and smiled.

"I know you didn't have much choice in it, but I'm glad you're here."

She smiled back and it warmed him. "I'm glad I'm here, too, and that we can be friends, even if we don't always see eye to eye."

"Me, too." It was a reflex, agreeing. Was he happy with being friends? What if he wanted more? He didn't know if that was even possible, but he liked the idea.

Aaron's unregistered phone rang. He drew it out and hit the button to answer Doug's call.

"Dude, you are not going to believe this."

Mackenzie saw the shift in his eyes as his concentration turned to the phone call. Aaron really thought leadership of his team made him responsible for his actions. Maybe in the army it did. But she couldn't help thinking sometimes awful things happened that couldn't be controlled.

She hadn't known her manager was involved with the Carosas, not until the police had told her. Witnessing the double murder of him and her security guard because her manager had been in over his head wasn't something she'd been able to avoid.

Wrong place, wrong time was right.

There was nothing she could do about that, but she had been able to control how she went forward. Recovering from her wounds, Mackenzie had agreed to testify, and her decision had shifted the power back into her hands.

Aaron was doing the same thing, except that his actions were chewing him up inside.

He sat on the arm of the chair, the phone to his ear. "What is it?" His eyes darkened further. "You're kidding me.…No.…Yeah, let me know."

He ended the call and looked at her. Maybe she didn't want to know, but she asked anyway. "What is it?"

"Eva is—" He blew out a breath. "I don't know how to soften the blow other than just saying it. Eva is Carosa's daughter—the Carosa who you put away, not his brother."

SEVENTEEN

Mackenzie's body tightened, but she couldn't help it. Her friend was the daughter of the man who had murdered two people and tried to kill her. Eva must have been just a teenager when Mackenzie had testified against him. Now Eva was tied up in all this and Eva's uncle was trying to kill Mackenzie.

The link was undeniable.

"Doug said there's a warrant out for her for the murder of U.S. Marshal Inspector Schweitzer. Eric's on the road to being cleared, but there's still no sign of Carosa. Doug and Sabine can't get involved in a federal manhunt, so they're coming here to help us."

Her mind was awash with the betrayal, and she could barely process what he was saying. "They are?"

Aaron nodded.

"We'll need to clean the place up, then, if there's going to be multiple people staying here."

"Mack—"

She went inside, grabbed some cleaning supplies and dumped them on the counter in the bathroom. Probably a good place to start. She ducked into the bedroom then and changed clothes. Once it was clean she'd be able to take a shower and wash off some of the grime of the past couple of days. When she was finally free of Carosa, she would book a hotel room and take a bath in one of those big spa tubs.

Maybe then she would be clean of the stink of being betrayed.

Mackenzie tied her hair up and got to scrubbing, taking all her frustration out on the grime on the tiles.

When she was almost done, his boot steps stopped at the door. "Wow, I feel sorry for the soap scum."

She glanced back over her shoulder. Aaron leaned against the doorjamb, clearly confused as to what was happening. Why couldn't she just say the words? *I hate my life.*

She was exhausted, physically and mentally, and had the feeling they were far from the end of all this. She didn't want to sleep, but she needed to. She didn't want to relive it all, though. In a vicious trick of the mind, the past would blend with the present and replay the scene back in the hotel room so long ago. Only now she would dream it was Aaron and not her security guard who jerked with the force of a bullet and collapsed into her so that they fell together to the ground.

She turned back to her scrubbing. "Why don't you get started on the kitchen?" Mackenzie shut her eyes at how curt she sounded, but he had to know she didn't want to talk. What? He could have space, but she couldn't?

"Are you mad at me?"

She huffed at the wall. "Why would I be?"

Now she sounded childish. Fabulous. She moved over and started on the next batch of tiles. The exhaustion of years of being hyperattentive to everything around her piled on top of days of running made her feel as though everything was dragging. But she wasn't going to sit around when they had guests coming.

"Eva's the one who betrayed you. Why are you taking it out on the tile?"

"It's not just her." She turned and pointed the sponge at herself. "I'm on the run from a guy who wants to kill me. I have no family, no friends—at least not anymore." And didn't that sound totally depressing? "I had to leave the life I've been building and I have no idea if I'm even going to be alive long enough to find out if I can build something from the nothing I have left."

His eyes softened and he stepped into the bathroom. "So you've resorted to cleaning as if your life depends on it? Sabine isn't going to care."

"I'm being a good host." She put one hand on her hip, only she still had the sponge in it and she was squeezing it, getting the shirt all wet. *Yuck.* She tossed it in the bath.

Aaron smiled. "I'll help, okay?"

She turned back. "Suit yourself."

Why was she taking it out on him? She wanted to kick herself, but that would be less pretty than this attitude. And also awkward. He was helping her, and she was snapping at him.

"Mackenzie—"

"I'm trusting you."

"I know that."

"With everything I have. Which, granted, isn't that much compared to some people, but still—"

"I *know.*"

She looked him in the eyes. "My safety, my future, everything that's good that I've done over the past sixteen years. All the things I've accomplished trying to be the kind of person I want to be. I'm putting all of it in your hands."

He nodded, and his eyes seemed to convey he understood the gravity of what she was saying. "I get all of that."

"That's all I need to know." She fingered the hem of the T-shirt. "It's not that I'm not grateful for what you've done…what you are doing. I am, you know that. I'm just saying…"

Aaron stepped closer to her. "I know what you're saying, and I'm going to do my best not to let you down. I can't make promises, I don't know the future and I won't pretend everything is going to be fine. I'd rather you were prepared for whatever the outcome will be. But I'll do everything I can to keep you safe until Carosa is caught."

"You might not know the future, but I believe God does. He'll keep me safe, even if that means using you to do it."

Before Aaron could check it, his body tensed. "Sure He will."

"You don't believe it?"

He shrugged. "I grew up going to church. But it's not as if it has to be a big deal, or anything. When I need God, I'll ask Him for help. Like after the sniper bullet grazed me, when I realized we were in really deep trouble. I prayed then because there was no other hope. But that was just in the moment."

Faith was an important part of life, and knowing how he saw it gave her more insight than she'd had before. "I'll be sure to ask Him now for the both of us."

Aaron gave her a short nod. Was he going to stay, say something more? But he blinked and whatever was between them dissolved.

She sighed to his back as he walked out of the bathroom. It hit her then. Just as she trusted him with everything, Aaron in turn was also giving everything to see that this was done. He had a life to go back to, and he must have considered the thought that something could happen that might jeopardize his ability to do his job.

What would she do if he was injured, or worse?

Mackenzie squared her shoulders. She could walk away now and spare herself the guilt, but she wouldn't last long before Carosa caught up with her. Maybe it was better that he was keeping this impersonal.

God, keep him safe. It doesn't matter what happens to me, just help Carosa be caught and don't let anything happen to Aaron. And help him to trust in You. He needs You.

He came back in then. Just walked straight up to her and put his arms around her shoulders. Mackenzie stilled, and then squeezed her eyes shut and put her arms around him, too. The simple hug touched her more than she ever would have thought possible.

They stayed like that for a while, before he said, "I'm sorry about Eva."

"Thank you." Mackenzie sniffed. "I'm sorry I'm being a pain."

Aaron chuckled, his chest shaking. "It's kind of cute, actually."

"You are not serious."

He touched her cheek then. He hadn't moved away. In fact, he might be even closer than he'd been a minute ago.

"Aaron—"

He touched his lips to hers, a kiss of comfort and companionship. Never mind that her stomach fluttered and she had to grab his elbows to steady herself.

Then he leaned back, and the corners of his lips curved up in a smile. "I'll go make up the extra beds and then get started on the kitchen."

Mackenzie watched him walk away. Aaron was a great distraction from the drama that was her life. There might be something between them, something she hadn't experienced before with anyone else. She didn't really know what to call it or what to do with it. But that didn't mean it was the real thing.

He seemed content to have their closeness be about friendship and him supporting her, and she loved that he was that kind of man. But even if he probably had a pretty good idea already, she still couldn't let him know just how much he affected her.

Because there was no way he felt the same way.

Aaron stepped outside a few hours later when Doug and Sabine pulled up in a silver car so out of place in the wilderness it was ridiculous. He eased the door closed without a sound and trotted down the steps. Something had awoken inside him when he'd kissed Mackenzie. It had been a whim, meant to comfort her in the face of Eva's betrayal, but he'd had to pull back before it quickly became a lot more meaningful.

She might be completely out of his league, but she made him want to try to be better. More open.

Now he was struggling with what to do, because Mackenzie had sparked something. And yet, women and his emotions weren't something that usually went together. Friendship maybe, but not love. He'd never understood the point of falling so deeply for someone that he lost his own identity in the process. Not to mention self-control. Turning into a blubbering, simpering mess just because a woman turned her sweetness toward him wouldn't make him a better soldier.

"Nice car."

Doug pulled him in for a hug that was just this side of painful and involved vigorous backslapping. "Fake ID. Rental. You know how it goes."

"Sure, but a hybrid?" Aaron gave Sabine a side hug.

She shot Doug a grin that he returned. Then Sabine smiled up at Aaron. "So where's Mackenzie?"

Doug nodded his shaved head. "Yeah, where is this mystery woman you're supposed to have abducted?"

"I persuaded her to take a nap. She was pretty wrung out."

"You look a little peaked yourself."

Aaron folded his arms. "Thanks, that was really helpful."

Sabine studied his face. "Oh, no. What happened?"

"Nothing." Did he really say that? As if Aaron was some junior-high kid with a secret crush to hide. "I should be asking you what you're doing. Care to share, since I'm not convinced you're just here to help out?"

Doug nodded to the cabin. "Let's head inside."

Aaron helped with their bags, and Doug hauled in two cardboard boxes. How long were they staying? He'd just set the bags down inside when Mackenzie poked her head out of the bedroom.

"You're up."

She swiped hair back from her face, her eyes still tired despite the nap.

"Sleep okay?"

"A little." She came over and stood by him, eyeing Doug with hesitation.

"Mackenzie, this is my former team leader, Doug Richardson. Sabine's fiancé."

They shook hands, and when she stepped back, Aaron put his arm around her shoulders. She glanced up at him, but he ignored it. "Why don't you just tell us the news that I can see on your face, Doug?"

The big man nodded. "Okay. But let's sit first."

"I'll put a pot of coffee on."

Mackenzie's attention zipped to Sabine. "Oh, the coffeepot…" Her nose wrinkled.

"Girl, tell me about it." Sabine laughed, pulling back the flaps of a box. "Brought my own."

Sabine drew out a coffeemaker and plugged it in. Aaron could appreciate this woman's idea of roughing it.

They made small talk while the mugs were all filled, and then Doug sighed.

"Just spill it already."

He shot Aaron a look. "Fine. Your girl here is all over the internet. The kids at the center must have figured out who she was, because they got a photo of her back when she was Lani and paired it with one taken recently. It was a nice gesture, 'Stay safe, we love you,' but the meme went viral, or whatever you call it. Now everyone knows who she really is." Doug sighed. "The media is running the story now."

Mackenzie strode to the window. The world outside was quiet. If she closed her eyes, she could almost forget other people even existed. *Or she could try.* It was a nice dream. Too bad it might get her killed.

Her identity was supposed to be a secret, and now everyone knew the shame she felt over the girl she had been. Wasn't it enough that Aaron and his friends knew she used to be Lani? Now the whole world would know the selfish girl who was Mackenzie's former life. She touched the glass with her fingertips and hung her head. Hadn't she paid enough?

Aaron made his way to her, but she couldn't deal with his comfort. If he was kind, she would lose it. This was all too embarrassing.

"No way."

Mackenzie glanced over at Sabine, ignoring Aaron now beside her. "What is it?"

Sabine was on a laptop, tapping away at the buttons.

She was probably touching base with contacts of hers who might be able to shed light for them on Carosa's whereabouts or something. Why did everyone seem to know what they were doing here except for Mackenzie?

"I don't believe this."

Mackenzie sighed. "What now?"

"See for yourself." Sabine turned the laptop on the table.

On the screen was a social media website. In the middle were two pictures side by side.

The left hand one was Lani Anders at the height of her career. The picture on the right was a snapshot of Mackenzie that had been taken from someone's phone. She remembered the day, one of the kids' seventeenth birthday. Mackenzie had brought cupcakes for everyone. She hadn't thought she was in any of the shots.

That must be what Doug had been talking about.

"So what? Isn't that what Doug just said? Why do we all have to look at it?"

Except that underneath the picture it now read, "$1,000,000.00, Dead or Alive."

EIGHTEEN

"Before it was nothing more than a nice message that might have outed your former identity. We weren't going to let anything happen to you, so it wasn't the end of the world. This meme has the same pictures, but someone doctored the words. Now it's a bounty for your capture."

"Or my death."

"Yes, that might pose a problem."

Mackenzie rolled her eyes. "Right, because Eva betraying me and mercenaries trying to abduct me wasn't enough of an issue, we needed things to get even more complicated. Why won't Carosa just leave me alone? Why is he sending all these people after me?"

"I actually have a theory about that."

Aaron and Doug both looked at Sabine, but it was Mackenzie who said, "What do you mean?"

"Well, maybe they're working together and they hired the mercenaries to get you. But what if Carosa didn't know where you were until now? It's also possible that everything that's happened to you since your tires were slashed is on Eva. She could have hired the mercenaries to get you and keep herself removed. She used Schweitzer and killed him. Maybe she's working with Carosa and she's going to deliver you to her uncle, or maybe she's after revenge for herself. Or both."

Sabine pushed back her chair and stood. "Look, no one knows we're here. If anyone did get the idea of chasing us down, there's enough ammo to take care of it."

The two men stood behind Sabine with similar looks of pity on their faces.

Mackenzie pressed a hand to the spot where she'd been shot. "I'm really trying not to be melodramatic here, but it's really hard. Everyone who sees that…"

"It's called a meme."

Mackenzie stared at the picture. The teenage face, the pop-star clothes. She squeezed her eyes shut. "They're all going to know who I was. And then Carosa's going to come and *kill me*."

Sabine frowned. "I used to listen to your music when I was in high school. It was pretty good. Is it really such a big deal if people find out who you were?"

"Yes."

"Why?"

Mackenzie's chest heaved. "Because I hate her. That spoiled, selfish little… She makes me so mad!" She pointed at the picture on screen. "The girl in that picture didn't care about anyone or anything but herself and what she could get. Her parents might not have cared one bit either, but that didn't excuse her behavior."

"You're ashamed." Sabine's words were soft.

"Of course I am!"

"I understand."

"You can't possibly—"

Sabine came over and caught Mackenzie's hand, squeezing some warmth into it, but Mackenzie couldn't let herself accept the comfort.

"God can wipe it away. He takes our sin and makes it as though it never happened. Do you believe that?"

"I'm a Christian. But it doesn't just disappear. I should know, because it's been years and it's still right there in my head. All the time." Mackenzie looked away. "Maybe your sin is as if it never happened, but mine isn't. It can't just get swiped away. There's no such thing as a clean slate."

"You're wrong." Sabine's voice wasn't full of judgment, but compassion.

Mackenzie blinked away the tears and looked back at her. "No."

Sabine reached for her hand. "You've been holding on to your guilt all this time. There's no need. Not when you can give it up, ask for forgiveness. It's not a trick that sends it away all of a sudden, it's living in grace. In God's love...for you."

The nausea from seeing herself on the computer for the world to see sat in her stomach like bad shrimp. She had to get rid of it, but she didn't know how to let go of the shame.

Sabine took a step closer to her. "Mackenzie, it's just—"

"No." She shook her head so fast everything blurred, and backed up into the hall. She couldn't let Aaron see her like this. It was too embarrassing. He was supposed to think she was good and strong, but she wasn't.

Aaron strode over. "Mackenzie. None of this changes—"

She slammed the door in his face.

Aaron rubbed his nose where the wood of the door had grazed it. He could hear the hitch in her breathing. She was crying. He shut his eyes and put a hand to the door, wishing he could shove his way through and get her to listen to reason. Was she really so embarrassed that they'd seen her picture?

His heart broke for this talented, beautiful woman, full

of promise and life. She had probably gotten used to fine things as a singer. Now she was a woman with a mission to help kids discover what they could do. What could he give her? And yet he couldn't ignore the way his heart seemed to have opened to her.

When it came down to it, she was as damaged as he was.

And yet Sabine seemed to think God could wash it away. As if it had never happened. Aaron was scared to believe that was even possible. What if he got his hopes up, and it didn't go anywhere?

Sabine sat at the kitchen table. "I didn't mean to upset her."

Doug laid his hand on her shoulder and squeezed.

Aaron forced his tired body across the room and lowered himself into a chair opposite her just as Doug did the same. "It wasn't your fault."

Sabine's mouth flicked up at the corners, but her gaze stayed on the computer screen. "It probably could've been better, though. But you know what I've learned from all the fights I've had with Doug? People get upset and angry because they care. It says something about how she feels about you that she's making sure she attacks you first because she's scared that what you're going to think will hurt."

Aaron winced. "I'm such an idiot."

Doug leaned back in his chair. "I could have told you that."

"Just you wait. I'll charm her yet, and you'll be eating your words."

Doug tipped his head back and laughed. How could this man have given up Delta Force? The guy was born for the military and yet he was interviewing for a private security company and building a life with Sabine. Ahead of them was marriage, a family.

Part of Aaron wanted that with Mackenzie.

He turned to Sabine. "Do you really believe that, what you said about living in God's grace?"

She nodded. "I know it's real, because it happened to me. I had to give up my preconceived notions of what faith is like, but now I know. It's freedom."

Doug put his arm around Sabine's shoulders. "Why don't you give us the update?"

Aaron was glad for the change in subject. Had his friend seen his discomfort and given him the out?

Still, Sabine's earnest belief and the change he'd seen in her since she met Doug all testified that God's love really did change a person.

Sabine reached for the laptop. "So the meme the kids did for Mackenzie is now some kind of twisted wanted poster."

Aaron's hands tightened into fists. "Maybe she should be on the first plane somewhere Carosa will never find her."

Doug's mouth twisted in a grin. "She's the one."

"What are you talking about?"

"Just something my dad said to me. I didn't believe he could've seen it until I saw the look on your face just now. This girl is it for you. She's the one."

"And I might have figured it out too late. I can try, but clearly she doesn't want me in her life past this joyful experience and I don't blame her. I haven't been thinking about her at all. Just myself."

Sabine squeezed his hand. "You're going through a lot, as well. You were trying to protect what you have left. And help Eric. You've been in a rough place, wondering what will happen when you get back and—"

Aaron shook his head. "Don't try to make me feel better."

"Mackenzie cares for you, and she thinks you don't feel the same. She's so scared of it, she's pushing you away the same way you pushed her away."

How had Sabine seen what he'd tried to keep to himself? "Mackenzie doesn't love me."

"Once she calms down and gives you a chance to explain, you'll see I'm right. Most of what that was is Mackenzie's own internal stuff. She's going through a lot with this."

"You think I don't know that?"

Sabine smiled. "But you are a guy, so I'm going to say it. You can get mad if you want, but she's dealing with a lot of guilt and shame over who she was when she was Lani Anders. It's been buried for a long time, but seeing that meme finally brought it out. She needs time to deal with her former identity being exposed. Then you can tell her how you feel."

"That's the problem. I've actually got to get her to listen."

Sabine tucked some hair behind her ear. "I get the impression she's lived so far under the radar she hasn't really let herself get close to anyone. A lot like the way you've never committed to anyone because you'd rather keep things light. It has to be hard to be confronted with all these feelings she's never had before…maybe even overwhelming."

Aaron rolled his eyes. "You know, you could actually try to be comforting."

Sabine burst into laughter. Doug swung his arm around his fiancée's shoulder. "That's my girl. She says it like it is."

"Yeah, no kidding." Aaron squeezed his neck. "Do you think I can do this relationship stuff? I've never really tried."

Doug shook his head. "You don't know for sure that you can't. I never believed a relationship would work, or that a woman would ever want to marry a soldier who's always gone. Now I'm in a different place. If she's the one for you, then you walk it together. You keep her in the loop, and she does the same for you. It's communication."

"Great. Communication was never my strength. You know I'm much better with action."

Sabine grinned. "I'm pretty sure she already figured that out."

He hoped so. This relationship stuff was complicated, and Aaron didn't want to mess it up. Mackenzie deserved his best effort if they were going to make something out of this.

But first, he had to get her to talk to him.

Two hours later, Mackenzie was trying to focus on a book Sabine had brought for her. Wrapped up in an over-size sweater she suspected was Aaron's, she was on the couch, cocooned and trying to pretend Carosa wasn't out there. As if the world was, in fact, a safe place to live.

The men had been in and out, patrolling the perimeter. They were acting as if this was a war zone, but maybe they just needed something to do. She sure did. The book was supposed to an epic wartime love story, but her heart wasn't in the right place to get lost in someone else's emotions.

Sabine ran out of the bedroom with her laptop. "Something's going on. It's all over the internet."

"I can't believe there's even a connection up here. We're in the middle of nowhere."

Sabine waved off her comment. "The guys set it up like that. There's a hut across the way that hunters sleep in occasionally, when they find it. The satellite internet goes to there and we're directly connected to it. But to intercept the signal you'd have to literally dig up the cable between that hut and this cabin and cut into it."

She set the laptop on the table. "It's all really technical, and I don't totally understand it. But suffice to say, there would be plenty of warning if someone tried to find us by tracing my IP address and trying to discover where I'm connecting to the internet from. And all it would lead them to is an even smaller, more run-down hut a quarter mile north of here."

"So what's going on?"

"Check it out." The screen blinked on the laptop and a local Phoenix news reporter with wide eyes came on. Shell-shocked. "Our sources at the police department say the vehicle was a black van."

A picture of the center came on screen. Mackenzie gasped and stepped back. That was her center. What was going on? The front windows of the building were shattered. Police and rescue vehicles blocked the street.

Mackenzie's heart jumped to her throat.

"Around nine-thirty last night gunmen opened fire on the Downtown Performing Arts Center, wounding several people, including minors. We're getting word of multiple injuries and that one girl—a teenager—is in critical condition." The news reporter cleared her throat. "We'll keep you updated as further information is related to us."

Mackenzie gasped. "No."

"I'm sorry." Sabine's eyes were wet even though she didn't know any of the kids.

Mackenzie took in a breath that shuddered through the band of emotion that had a lock on her chest. Just children. Her children. In harm's way because of her.

"I'm so sorry, Mackenzie."

"I have to go."

"No—"

"I have to be there. Sabine, I can't just sit here. My kids are in the hospital. They got shot at last night."

"They're getting help, Mackenzie."

"That's not good enough!"

Aaron stepped through the door. Mackenzie was freaked. "What's going on?"

Sabine answered, "Someone shot up the center. There are wounded kids, and some of them in the hospital."

He went straight to Mackenzie. She tried to flee, but he caught her and wrapped her in his arms. When her legs buckled, he swept her up and carried her out to the porch swing. Keeping her in his hold as he sat, Aaron rubbed her back while she cried.

So much weight she carried. There wasn't much more she could take before she broke in a way he was worried she'd never come back from.

"I'm going to help you through this, Mackenzie. I'm not going anywhere."

Aaron closed his eyes and kept rubbing Mackenzie's back, though her crying had tapered off to little sobs. If he gave everything over to God, that meant giving God control of his relationships, too. Did God want Aaron to risk everything he had that way? Everyone else seemed to believe it was the right thing to do, but did that mean he had to adopt it, also?

Mackenzie would be worth it. He didn't doubt that. But if he were to risk the pain of heartbreak and things with Mackenzie went bad… He blew out a breath. When it was over, there wouldn't be much left of Aaron worth speaking of, and he'd failed enough for this lifetime. Franklin's blindness was proof of that.

He could see how God could use Mackenzie as a blessing in his life to make it richer. Yet something in him still held back to the point he pushed her away. Was he strong enough to overcome that? Because while it took a lot to risk his life every day as a soldier…risking his heart?

That was a whole different story.

NINETEEN

Mackenzie rotated the handle slowly and eased the door open so as not to wake Sabine, who was asleep in the other bed. Her head was still stuffed up from crying, and she was exhausted but couldn't seem to be able to fall asleep. All she did was lie in bed and think about the kids from the class she'd supervised the last day she was there. Those frustrating traits of obstinacy and the air of bad attitude that surrounded so many of them now seemed almost endearing.

They'd suffered so much already in their lives. Neglect, poverty and some even abuse. They hadn't needed this, too.

Mackenzie crept into the living room. It was lit by the yellow light above the oven, and she could make out the couch and coffee table. The rug was soft under her bare toes, and she curled up in the armchair, knees to her chest with the sleeves of her sweater pulled down over her hands.

When was all this going to be over? Would there even be a center to go back to? The front of the building had been destroyed, and several of the kids were wounded. Mackenzie squeezed her eyes shut for the millionth time, but there were no more tears. It was all her fault for trying to help them. For not being satisfied with living a simple, quiet life.

She'd tried to help them realize how talented they were, but all she'd done was put them in harm's way.

She'd walked away from her life once. She could do it again, but it would still cost her to begin anew. Another house in another city surrounded by new people and places; having to put down roots all over again, always prepared to run at any time. Carosa would still be out there, and Eva would still want revenge for her father's death, so she'd have a new WITSEC handler. It was like a sentence, life in prison, but without the locks and bars.

Would she ever be free?

Mackenzie laid her cheek on the back of the chair and stared out the window. The night sky was still, the trees outside unmoving as they enveloped her in a silence that meant she could block out the rest of the world. Pretend there weren't people out there who wanted her dead.

Something shifted, and she turned. Aaron was on the couch, sitting up. He pushed aside a blanket and came to sit on the edge of the coffee table in front of her, rubbing sleep from his eyes. His white T-shirt stretched across his chest, showing the tone of his arms and making her mouth dry. "Mackenzie?"

In the dark she could just make out a small smile on his face. He looked exhausted from being on alert protecting her, another casualty of her selfishness. "You okay?"

Mackenzie looked back at the window. There was no point in getting used to having him there. She needed to know how to live without him.

"Thinking about leaving?"

The longing she felt was there in his voice, too. Mackenzie looked back at him. This wasn't going to last, so why was he acting as if it would bother him to see her leave?

"You look so lost. I wish I knew what to do, how to help."

Mackenzie had to not come on too strong. Just because Aaron was being open with her didn't mean he was willing to accept everything she had to give. What if he pulled away again? She needed to keep her own feelings locked up tight. He couldn't know that she was falling for him, because if he left there was no way she'd be able to come back from it. She had to guard her heart.

His gaze roamed over her face, but he didn't seem satisfied. He sighed. "Couldn't sleep?"

"I've never slept that well. At first it was dreams of watching Daniel die and seeing Carosa's eyes when he shot me."

Aaron bit his lip. "Daniel?"

"He was my head of security. We were friends, and I foolishly hoped for more. Then Carosa shot my manager, and Daniel and I walked in just in time to see it happen. Carosa shot Daniel before he could fire back, and then shot me."

Mackenzie touched her fingers to the spot just under her right shoulder. "Right here. It went through pretty cleanly, but left a nice hole in my lung. I actually stopped breathing before he left the hotel room. The person in the next room heard the shots and someone got the paramedics there quickly enough to bring me back. All because my manager didn't pay his debt to the Colombians."

Aaron's head tipped to one side. "It sounds as though God kept you here for a reason."

Mackenzie stilled. "Why would He do that?"

"All the kids you brought into the center. You've made a difference in each of their lives, something they needed. It's an amazing thing you've done with them, giving them confidence in their talents and making them feel loved and valued. And me…"

"You?"

"You've made a difference in me, Mackenzie."

He might be able to claim that, but the kids wouldn't be able to say it about her. Not now that she had destroyed their lives, too. A tear slid down her cheek.

"Hey." Aaron wiped the moisture away with his thumb. "Don't be sad. It's a good thing. I like the idea that God knew I needed you in my life. I care about you a lot. More than I've ever cared about a woman before."

Mackenzie shook her head. "Don't say that. I'm not who you think I am. Not anymore. The center is gone, and I'll be gone, too, still running from Carosa. What's the point in hiding out here if he's going to keep killing people until he finds me? Or Eva? Maybe she'll be the one I'm looking over my shoulder for for the next sixteen years. It's never going to end, Aaron."

"Of course it will. What do you think we're doing here?"

"Hiding?"

"More like mounting a defensive position on high ground while we wait for the enemy to attack."

"So we just sit here for however long it takes?" Could she even do that? "I won't ask you all to put your lives on hold for me. It's not fair to any of you." If something happened to them, she would never forgive herself.

"There are just too many ways to track someone that it's virtually impossible to hide anymore. Not with all the technology we have, or Carosa's resources. But I'm not giving up, Mackenzie, and I'm not going to let anyone hurt you. I've found something here, with you. And I'm not leaving until I know how it's going to turn out."

Aaron was ready to tell her everything. He'd been satisfied for a long time with shallow relationships that didn't force him out of his comfort zone. But something was missing. He'd been living life to the fullest, pushing the boundaries of what he was capable of physically—playing hard at his job and on vacations rock climbing and skydiving, but that wasn't life.

In fact, those things seemed almost meaningless. They challenged his strength but didn't let him feel anything past the rush of adrenaline. For the first time he actually felt something—compassion for Mackenzie's situation, and then coming to know her heart and her strength it grew to more than that.

It had changed him. He was proud of her achievements. And knowing the heart behind everything she did was about helping troubled kids, well…

Aaron had to admit, that uncomfortable feeling in his chest was love for her. Love she would be hesitant to accept, feeling as if she didn't deserve it when nothing could be further from the truth. She was an amazing woman.

"Mackenzie—"

The front door of the cabin opened and Doug rushed in. "The hut has been breached." Aaron stood while he strode over and set his night-vision goggles on the table. Doug stood straight and tall, battle ready. "Four men at the other cabin. They found the source of the signal and they're headed up the mountain now on foot, spread out in formation ready to take this cabin."

"Armed?"

"They're not carrying water guns." Doug went to the bedroom door and knocked before he cracked it open and stuck his head in to where Sabine was sleeping. "It's time."

Seconds later, Sabine came out with her pistol. Doug took a rifle from on top of the fridge and tossed it to Aaron before he grabbed the other for himself. Aaron checked the weapon, making sure it was loaded and ready to fire.

Mackenzie came over, her eyes darting between his face and weapon. "What's going on?"

"The mercenaries are on their way. They'll have the back exits covered, and they'll be prepared. They're pros, Mackenzie. But four of them don't outmatch Doug, Sabine and I. Remember how you said you were trusting me with everything you had? Well, I need you to do that now, even though it's going to get scary. Whatever happens, just keep your head down, and if I tell you to do something, you don't hesitate. Got it?"

She bit her lip and nodded. He didn't like going back to giving terse orders, but she looked so scared it would surely make her hesitate when she needed a clear head.

If the guys coming up the mountain were the same ones who had been chasing them for days, they were likely supremely angry and looking for revenge. He figured this wasn't so much about their doing the job anymore, but about saving face after being bested by Sabine and outsmarted by Aaron. They didn't know Sabine's skills were off the charts since she'd been trained by the CIA.

Aaron looked around, satisfied they had what they needed to keep Mackenzie from being taken again. This time he wouldn't have to watch her walk away.

He looked at her again. "Trust me."

The words sounded far away. She blinked at the weapons all around her. The magnitude of firepower in the room was overwhelming, and she backed into the kitchen until she hit a chair. She grasped it with trembling fingers and sat down, breathing deeply. It was like some Wild West siege scene in a movie. And everyone except her had a gun.

This was her life now. Not just running and hiding, but fighting. And the fact these people were prepared to kill in order to keep her safe? Her brain wouldn't quit spinning. They could die. Or one of them could be seriously hurt.

Trust me.

Could she do that when she knew what loss felt like? Carosa might take Sabine, too—a good person who was only here because she cared what happened to Mackenzie. And Doug, about to get married and spend the rest of his life with the woman he loved. The price was too high. There was no way she was worth their lives.

Years ago, she craved being the focus of what was going on. Lani would have soaked up the attention, but Mackenzie didn't know what she would do if something happened to one of these precious people, so honorable that they would risk their lives. For her.

Sabine and Doug stood beside the windows, their bodies angled to scan the night outside. Aaron walked through the cabin, turning off lights—except for the light of the laptop on the table. Each of them was completely focused on what was happening. Aaron's movements were precise, as though he'd done this a million times. He'd trained for stuff like this? It was unreal.

On the computer screen, a window blinked. It disappeared, and then flickered and appeared again.

Sabine spoke, "Bogey at two o'clock."

Doug didn't move. "Me, too. I've got one at ten o'clock."

Aaron brushed by Mackenzie, nodding at the computer. "Shut that off." He moved to the fridge, pulled it out and yanked the plug from the socket in the process. He dragged the appliance across the floor and pushed it up against the door, blocking that entrance, and brushed off his hands. "The other two are probably around back. What are they waiting for?"

Mackenzie clicked on the pop-up window. It was an instant message. But from whom?

You in the cabin. Send out the girl and no one has to die.

TWENTY

She should just close the lid. Mackenzie didn't want anyone to die, but what else was she supposed to do? The three of them were trained. This was what they did, so she should just trust that they would keep her safe. And yet, none of them knew what the outcome would be. Mackenzie wanted to pray, but all she could think was what she would do if one of them was hurt. Or killed.

Just the girl. That's all I want.

Her fingers hovered over the keys for a moment. She tossed aside the prick of doubt at what she was about to do and typed, If I come out, you have to leave them alone.

The response came almost immediately: You have my word.

Eva. She must be out there, if the mercenaries were hers. Or it could be Carosa. Mackenzie should have known that neither of them would leave it to chance after so many failed attempts to capture her. But what was the alternative? Live a life where every crazy person came out of the woodwork to collect the million-dollar reward? Never having a moment's peace? Her dreams of home and a family couldn't be part of her future, and she just needed to accept that. But that didn't mean Doug, Sabine and Aaron had to.

Mackenzie looked over at the living room. Doug and Sabine still had their attention on the front windows. Aaron would be a problem. He stood at the entrance to the back hall, his eyes on the rear door. The only other option was… the bathroom window. She prayed it wasn't locked.

Mackenzie typed the message that would seal her fate: I'm coming out the side window.

She didn't wait for the response. It didn't matter anymore that Eva and Carosa would win. Her life wasn't more important than three people who would go on without her because they didn't need to have their lives, their missions, cut short.

When she stood, her knees shook. Mackenzie willed strength into her legs to carry out what she was about to do. She slipped on her shoes and went to Aaron. "I have to use the bathroom." She didn't meet his eyes, and hoped he wouldn't hear the tremble in her voice.

"Right now?"

She prayed he was too honorable to come between a woman and her personal needs.

"Be quick."

Mackenzie pushed out a breath through tight lips and looked up. "I just want to say thank you. For everything."

He frowned. "Mackenzie—"

She backed up and pushed open the bathroom door. "I really have to go."

"Leave the light off. You don't want to draw attention to yourself."

Mackenzie closed the door and squeezed her eyes shut. Waiting a minute, she flushed the toilet, using the sound to cover the scrape of her opening the window. She gritted her teeth and pulled herself up to the frame.

A man dressed in black appeared out of nowhere. He wore those weird goggles like Doug had done, covering his eyes. Green-and-brown paint was slashed across his face in wide swipes, and he had a huge gun in his hands. He let go with one hand and motioned for her to come.

Mackenzie kept her eyes on the outside. If she looked back at the closed bathroom door, knowing Aaron was just beyond it, she would lose her nerve. This was the best way, the only way. She held her breath and crawled out. The night air was frigid enough to cut through her sweatshirt and yoga pants and make her shiver. Breath puffed out in white clouds in front of her as she crossed the open stretch of grass to the soldier.

When she got near, he grabbed her upper arm in a tight grip. She sucked in a breath, but he didn't loosen his grasp, just pulled her along. Farther and farther from the house.

He pressed a button on his vest. "I have her. Get rid of the others."

He kept going, too fast so that she stumbled to keep up. "What do you mean—"

Gunfire erupted behind her. Long spurts from the weapons of the men hired to collect her for Carosa.

"She gave me her word she wouldn't hurt them."

The soldier shook his head, goggles still covering his eyes and focused on the path they were cutting through the brush.

"She promised me." Mackenzie didn't even know who had sent these men for her.

"And you believed it? No one is trustworthy, least of all who you're dealing with." He snorted. "Case in point, we dumped the woman since the drug lord's son pays better. So it's off to Carosa you go."

Mackenzie looked back at the house. Everything was still and quiet. So fast. Were they dead?

"Don't bother looking. No one will be coming for you this time."

She stumbled and went down on one knee to the cold, hard ground. He jerked her arm so hard she cried out. They walked and walked through the brush. Her limbs grew stiff, the feeling permeating all the way through to her heart.

She felt nothing but the cold.

Aaron, Sabine and Doug were all dead because of her. Everything she had done was for nothing, a complete failure of her effort to do the right thing.

Aaron smashed the sole of his boot into the door, just beside the lock. It swung open, hit the bath and bounced back splintered. The window was open.

Mackenzie was gone.

"No!"

Gunfire discharged like a deafening wave of fireworks. He dived to the floor as shards of wood and insulation rained down on his head. He peered out at the living room. Doug and Sabine had done the same thing. Both were prone with their arms covering their heads as bullets peppered the front of the cabin. Doug brushed a splinter from his ear and crawled to his fiancée.

The front door was kicked in and the fridge was shoved aside. Aaron lifted his weapon and fired, the sound muffled to his ringing ears. His aim was off, but he succeeded in distracting the two men and giving Doug and Sabine time to rally. They got to their feet and surged at the two mercenaries hand to hand, almost in sync. Before he turned away, Sabine already had her man on the floor.

Aaron raced for the back door at the end of the hall, hoping and praying he wasn't too late. Carosa must have gotten to her. Maybe she was just outside and he could reach her in time.

He flew out the door and scanned the area with his weapon ready. Black earth and dark sky, lots of stars and a full moon meant good visibility. Once his eyes adjusted, he would be able to see as clear as if it were day. But she wasn't here. It had been only minutes since she'd entered the bathroom, but Mackenzie was as good as long gone.

Footsteps shuffled through the shrubs behind him, and before Aaron could turn and face his attacker, someone slammed into him. He hit the dirt with at least two hundred fifty pounds on top of him and the breath burst from his lungs. Aaron rolled, using the momentum to push the guy off so he could gain his feet.

The guy looked ex-military but didn't hold his stance like any of the Special Forces branches Aaron was aware of. More like a grunt who thought too highly of himself. Left-handed. He punched before the guy had straightened, catching him off guard. But not for long.

The mercenary swung with the butt of his rifle. Aaron ducked and punched again. The exhilaration of a fair fight rushed through him, lighting his nerve endings. With the hyperawareness that came from intense combat, Aaron deflected and drove forward with the force of his strength and training and pinned the guy on the ground.

"Where is she?"

The mercenary didn't answer. He labored for breath under the force of Aaron's knee and shifted to get a grip, but Aaron was determined.

"Where are you supposed to take her?"

The guy looked up. His face morphed in to a sneer. "I have no idea. Payment upon delivery, you know how it goes."

"Unfortunately, I do."

Aaron released his grip and the guy slumped to the ground, wheezing. Sickness churned his stomach as he got up. This guy was nothing more than a thug for hire without an honorable bone in his body. And Mackenzie had willingly gone with them, most likely to her death.

Who did that?

Doug raced out the back door with Sabine right behind him. Blood trickled from a cut on his cheek.

"You guys okay?"

Sabine was out of breath. "We're good. Where is she?"

Aaron lifted his hands and let them fall back to his sides. "They got to her."

"What?"

"I should have known." He kicked at a rock on the ground with every bit of strength he could muster. "She climbed out the bathroom window and just gave herself up to them. I knew when she said thank-you that something was off. I knew it. I should have asked what was wrong, but there wasn't any time and I wanted her to be quick."

How had she duped him so thoroughly? What made her get that idea in her head in the first place? He had no idea why someone would make that decision. There must have been something to trigger it, because it wouldn't have come out of nowhere.

Aaron's hands curled into fists and he growled. *The computer.*

"What is it?"

Aaron ignored Doug's question and raced inside, down the hall to the kitchen table. The computer's screen was completely smashed, a hole in the middle where a bullet had torn through it. The answers to all of this might have been right there, and now there was no way to find out, to understand why Mackenzie had walked away.

Why she'd left him.

Aaron ran his hand down his face. For all his trying to be honest with her, wanting to share his feelings so that she knew where he stood, at the end of the day Mackenzie had chosen not to trust him. His heart ached, the feeling so foreign he wanted to rip the thing out of his chest just to be rid of the pain.

He sank to the floor. The one woman in the world he wanted to understand him, and it was as if she didn't even care. Why else would she have left him without saying anything?

Doug crouched beside him. "Dude, talk to me."

"She didn't trust me."

Sabine's forehead crinkled. "I don't think it was about a lack of trust."

"She said goodbye to me and I didn't even realize." Aaron pinched the bridge of his nose. "She thought she didn't have anything else to live for, so she walked to her death like some kind of condemned prisoner. No fighting. Everything was over so she might as well give up. Who does that?"

Sabine crouched on his other side. "Someone who'll sacrifice themselves to save the person they love."

"We were fine. We're all trained for this, and she knew that. It doesn't make any sense."

"To you." Sabine squeezed his shoulder. "Because you knew we had the skills to survive. All Mackenzie knew was that men were coming for her—just her. We were surrounded. She acted, albeit unwisely. She should have shared what she was planning. But she probably didn't because you'd never have allowed it."

Doug scoffed. "Of course he wouldn't."

"Why? You both sacrifice every day, putting your lives on the line to make the world safer. Why shouldn't Mackenzie do the same?" Sabine glanced between the two men as though what she said was the most obvious thing in the world.

A smile curled Doug's lips.

Aaron squeezed his eyes shut. "She thought she was saving us."

"Seems like that to me."

He looked up at his friends. "So how do we save her?"

The more miles they drove, the more certain Mackenzie was of where they were going. In the early hours of the morning they pulled up outside the Downtown Performing Arts Center. The huge building looked ominous, lit by the glow of streetlamps that highlighted the boarded-up front windows. For years she'd loved coming here, knowing she was finally doing something good with her life.

The idea of going inside made her want to scream and rage against the injustice of simply being in the wrong place at the wrong time—and getting shot in the chest for it. Why couldn't Carosa just leave her be?

She flexed her hands. The tight, thin plastic of the tie her captors had used again cut into the skin of her wrists. The soldier walked around the car and opened her door from the outside, the only way it could be opened. She'd learned that the hard way from attempting to jump from the vehicle after he'd forced her into it.

Being laughed at was not one of her favorite things.

Mackenzie sat in the car until he reached in and hauled her out by the arm. She bit her lip, not giving him the satisfaction of knowing he'd hurt her. The street was deserted. It was as though every living being had run for cover. Marched into the building by the force of the large man's will, she scanned every corner for help. Inside was just as desolate.

The soldier shoved her, and she stumbled into the room.

Carosa stood there, arms folded across the silk shirt he was wearing. A gold chain hung around his neck. Khaki pants and brown loafers completed an outfit that looked more like something a used car salesman would wear than the middle-aged son of a senile drug lord.

Where was Eva? She'd assumed her former friend would be here, wanting her piece of Mackenzie, too. Or that Eva had been the one bringing Mackenzie to her uncle.

His eyes fixed on her. They were so much like his brother's dirt-colored ones that for a moment she was back in that hotel so many years ago. But she wasn't going to back down.

Carosa sneered. "Very good. Now we finish this."

TWENTY-ONE

Mackenzie held her body tight against the trembles that stretched down to her toes. *God, help me. This is so much worse than stage fright. Why did I think I could fight it?* Except that this whole thing had come about because of her decision to sacrifice herself for Aaron and his friends.

She hadn't prayed once or asked God to help her do the right thing. So what right did she have to cry out to Him now? Mackenzie hung her head. The weight of guilt bore down like a thousand pounds on her shoulders.

"And my money?"

She looked up, surprised to see the soldier still in the room.

Carosa crossed to them. "I have one more job for you." He handed the soldier two small packages. "Place these at opposite ends of the building. Ground level. And if I was you, I wouldn't accidentally drop one."

"That'll cost you double."

"Done." Carosa motioned to the door with his chin. "The money will be wired to your account. Once you've placed the bombs, you may leave."

"Whatever, man. Just so long as I get paid."

Mackenzie watched him saunter out, and then turned back to Carosa.

"Now the real fun begins," he said.

She backed up, but he grabbed hold of her bound hands and pulled her across the room. She wanted to kick and scream, but the strength had evaporated from her limbs. Her pulse pounded in her fingers. She was pushed to sitting and her brain spun, unable to latch on to a single thread of thought.

Where was help? Who was going to come and save her? Did she even have the right to expect a rescue? She had to face the fact that it was possible no one would find her here. She needed the courage to fight, despite how bad the situation looked. She had to be strong if she was going to get herself out of this alive.

"You won't get away with this."

"Thanks, Sabine. I owe you big-time for this."

Aaron ended the call and threw the phone in the cup holder. He raced through surface streets across the heart of Phoenix, already certain where Mackenzie was even before Sabine confirmed it for him.

"What did she say?"

He shot Doug a glance. "She hacked Eva's email account. There's a bunch of messages between her, Schweitzer and Carosa. Apparently she was playing them off against each other. In one of the emails, Carosa said he's going to end things tonight at the place where it started. She said it reads like a suicide note."

"The place where it started—wouldn't that be the hotel where Carosa's brother killed Mackenzie's manager and security guy?"

Aaron shrugged. "That's what I thought at first, but there's no way he could get her to a hotel in New York if it's all going down tonight."

Doug glanced out the window. "How far away are we?"

"I'm driving as fast as I can."

"I'm just saying, there's no time to lose."

"You think I don't know that?"

"Fine. It's just, I've been there. I know what it feels like to worry about the woman you love until you finally see her. The relief when you do is about the best thing you can ever feel. Until then…not so fun."

"Oh, thanks. That's helpful." Aaron made a right turn so fast that Doug grabbed the dash to brace himself.

"That's me, Mr. Helpful."

Two minutes later they pulled onto the street that backed onto the center. Aaron cut between a law office and a restaurant and parked. They scaled a chain-link fence and sprinted forward. At the back door of the center, Doug gestured that he would lead and go right and that Aaron should go left.

They crept inside, and Aaron searched the halls with his gun drawn. He passed Mackenzie's office, dark now, and kept going to the end of the hall, where he came upon one of the mercenaries. He was crouched, doing something with a package.

Aaron hit the man on the back of the head with the butt of his gun. The soldier slumped to the ground, leaving the package exposed. And beeping. Aaron set his gun down, pulled a pocket tool out and clipped one of the wires.

Silence.

He blew out a breath, grabbed his gun and sent Doug a text to watch out for bombs on the other side of the building. Faint voices drifted to him from a room—a man's and Mackenzie's. He had to get to her before he lost her forever. Aaron crept toward the door.

* * *

Mackenzie tried to sound confident while inside she was shaking. "Do you want to end up in jail like your brother?"

"What if I do? What business is it of yours?"

She stared at Carosa in shock. "But why? Are you going to go after the man who killed your brother in that prison riot?"

"That scum was dead the day he laid a hand on my brother. My only lament is that it was not me who stuck him like a pig." Carosa pulled a chair over and sat with his knees only inches from hers. "Now that you'll be dead, too, I find I've lost interest in the chase. There is little left to live for, you see."

"You're planning on dying with me."

"Clever girl."

"You don't want to be with your niece?"

His eyes flickered with something that actually looked like surprise. "My what?"

"Eva. Your niece. She works for me. She's the reason you found me."

"You lie. I have no relatives save my decrepit father. And this Eva you're talking about is nothing but a stupid girl who shouldn't have stuck her nose in something not her business just because she needed money. But I'll deal with her, too."

"She's your niece."

He shook his head. "Impossible."

"I'm telling you the truth."

"And I should believe you?"

There was movement in the doorway, but when Mackenzie looked no one was there. Just wishful thinking that Aaron had found her when there was no possible way he could have. She would die here, at the whim of this psycho. Alone. Just like always.

Unless she could buy some time.

Mackenzie pushed aside the rush of cold. "I'd rather you didn't kill me. I mean, who's going to clean up the mess?"

Carosa shifted in his chair. "I feel as if I should say a few words to mark this occasion. Since it will be the last either of us ever sees on this earth."

"How about I say something?"

Mackenzie gasped. He was really here. Aaron had found her.

Carosa shot up out of his chair, his gun pointed at Aaron. She squeezed her eyes shut, unable to bear the sight of the man she loved being killed. A gun fired and someone fell, but it wasn't Aaron. In front of her lay the gruesome sight of Carosa's dead body, and beyond Aaron, at the door, stood a woman.

Eva had shot Carosa.

"Drop your gun."

Her former friend pointed a gun at his head. Aaron crouched and placed his weapon on the floor. He spun and his leg flew out, catching Eva behind her knees with a swipe. She yelped and fell backward, and her gun fired.

Mackenzie screamed. The bullet hit the wall behind her head.

Aaron grabbed the side of Eva's neck, and Mackenzie took in deep breaths, not wanting to see Aaron kill someone she'd thought of as a friend, even if Eva had betrayed her. But Aaron held on to her until she was limp but still breathing, and he set her on the floor.

Then he pulled Mackenzie to her feet and his breath came warm on her ear. "Mackenzie." The sound of it was like the chiding of a small child. "Why did you leave like that? Didn't I promise I would keep you safe?"

A sob worked its way from her throat, followed by another until the tears flowed freely. Aaron cut the ties and freed her. He massaged her hands until blood circulated again and then wrapped his arms around her.

"You came."

His chest rumbled with laughter. "You doubted me?"

"I wouldn't let myself believe it. I thought I didn't deserve to be saved."

Aaron drew her away from him and touched his warm palm to her cheek. "You don't ever have to doubt me. I'll always be there for you."

Undeserved, just like God's grace. She didn't have to do anything to earn it. God would always love her no matter what she did or the kind of person she was. She wanted to laugh now, thinking of the years she'd spent trying to prove she was worthy of His love.

Here in front of her was all the proof she needed. Not because of the atonement she'd done, but for who she was. God had taken the bad and used it to make Mackenzie's life into something beautiful.

Aaron's face dipped until his lips touched hers. It was just starting to get interesting when his phone rang.

"This had better be good, dude." His smiled dropped. "You're kidding me." He hung up, already pulling her out of the room. "Doug couldn't disarm the other bomb. We have to get out of here. It's going to go off."

"Not so fast."

Aaron's body froze. Mackenzie looked over his shoulder as he turned. Eva. She was up on her feet with her gun pointed at them again. "Neither of you is going to get out of here alive."

Aaron spun around. She'd been down. Out. How could he have been so careless as to assume Eva was no longer a threat? In his haste to get to Mackenzie, he'd made a rookie mistake. One they were all going to pay for.

He straightened and stared down the barrel of Eva's gun. "The whole building's going to blow in a second. We have to get out of here or we'll all be dead."

"You think I'm just going to let her walk away after what she did to my family? I've been waiting years to get back at her without it looking as if I did it! I didn't hire gang bangers to kill you in a drive-by and then bring in mercenaries to abduct you only to have them double-cross me…" She dissolved into a rant. "All that work to look innocent and they go and ruin it. And I'm *not* leaving just because you say there's a bomb. Nice try." Eva's lip curled. "I'm not about to leave the two of you—"

A boom shook the building like an earthquake, gone in a flash. Eva's confident facade slipped. The building creaked and shuddered. Mackenzie screamed as the room started to list to one side. Eva's eyes darted around the room. Aaron seized the opportunity, rushing her when her focus was elsewhere, and grabbed for her gun a split second before her eyes came back to him.

She fired off rounds, one after the other, while they grappled for the weapon. Aaron had to keep it away from being aimed at Mackenzie and not get shot himself, but he managed it. Finally he had control of the gun, his elbow pinning Eva to the floor.

Chairs and tables slid across the room to the lowest point. Metal shrieked as it contorted, and drywall cracked and broke apart around them. Aaron glanced at Mackenzie and a sharp right hook slammed into his temple. Sparks filled his vision and he was pushed aside as Eva scrambled to the door and ran.

Aaron shook off the daze. They had to get out of there now.

He worked his way to Mackenzie and grabbed her hand. "Come on!"

Mackenzie ran with every bit of strength she could muster through the center's maze of halls. She glanced back. Eva was running in the other direction. The floor rumbled, and Eva fell through, screaming.

Mackenzie turned back just as Aaron jumped a hole where the floor had fallen away, hauling her with him. Twice they had to backtrack for a way out that was clear of debris. Aaron pulled her along, his speed giving her an extra boost so she took oversize steps.

Air rushed down the hall and whipped at her hair. Aaron's step faltered, and he turned. The look on his face went from intense concentration to wide-eyed. The floor began to shake, and yet another boom of thunder rent the air.

Another bomb?

"Secondary explosion."

Mackenzie didn't realize she'd spoken aloud until he answered her.

The floor splintered beneath her feet, and then she was falling. Aaron's grip tightened until it almost crushed the bones in her hand. They dropped through the floor into the basement.

Mackenzie slammed into the concrete and her ankle buckled beneath her weight. She cried out, but the sound was muffled with the roar of the explosion. Aaron hauled her up, and they kept moving forward. His hand was outstretched as he felt their way through. It was the boiler room.

The building shuddered and fell around them, encasing them in a concrete tomb. Aaron shoved her through a door, into another room sided by thick cinder block walls. Mackenzie stumbled and fell.

With her free hand outstretched, she scrambled around and watched as Aaron fell under the weight of the water heater. His head hit the concrete, and the heater slammed onto his lower body. Ash rained down on her, the hot air from the explosion all around them, sucking the moisture from the room.

Mackenzie collapsed.

TWENTY-TWO

God, help us. Mackenzie scanned the dark of the space they were in. The building creaked and groaned, and she heard the distant sound of sirens and people shouting. Help was here. They just had to last long enough to be dug out. But how long would that take? She scrambled to stand under the highest point, which was barely above her head.

"Help! We're trapped in the basement!" She screamed until her voice broke and then crumpled to her knees, coughing. "You have to help us."

Aaron moaned and shifted under the weight of the water heater. Mackenzie winced. When she'd first purchased it, it had taken two men to muscle the thing off the cart and into place. A moment that had marked the building of her new life; now it was all destroyed.

Mackenzie crawled to him and brushed a smudge of dirt from his forehead. It smeared. "Aaron." She whimpered. "You have to wake up."

He didn't move.

"Aaron, I need you to wake up."

A groan came from deep in his throat.

"I'm right here, Aaron. Someone will get us out, I can hear them. Only you have to stay with me. Don't leave. I can't do this without you. That…that's not life."

He grunted and shifted as though he was trying to fight the pain. Maybe he shouldn't do that. "Lie still. They'll get us out, okay?"

Life without him would be…desolate and empty. Like it was down there in the boiler room, nothing but smoke and rubble and the remnants of something that used to be great. She refused to drown in despair. That wasn't going to help them get out of there. Instead Mackenzie picked her way to the nearest wall and felt around.

"Call for help."

She rushed back to his side. "Aaron."

He grunted and held up his phone.

There was a deep crack in the screen and no power. Her stomach turned over. What good was technology now?

All around them were beams of wood and bits of what used to be the walls of her building, and the concrete walls of the basement. "It's going to take them forever to dig us out of here."

"Don't have forever."

She moved back to him and crouched low so her face was close to his. Her heart broke at the stark pain in his eyes. "Tell me."

"Can't breathe."

The heater wasn't on his upper body, so his back was clear. Had he fallen wrong? Circling around his head, she went to his other side.

There was a pool of blood beside his torso.

She looked, but couldn't find where it was coming from. At least it wasn't a lot of blood. But if he couldn't breathe, that didn't mean anything good. Right?

"Aaron—"

"Back to me."

She did as he asked, coming back around so he could see her face. Her eyes were full of tears, but she didn't hide them. One spilled out and tracked down her face. She swiped away the grit.

"Talk."

"You want me to distract you?"

The nod of his head was the slightest of movements she'd have missed if she wasn't looking right at him.

She took a deep breath and exhaled. "I don't know what to say." How precious it was, just to be able to breathe. Air was something easily taken for granted, but the ability to simply inhale oxygen was a gift.

God, You made our bodies, You made Aaron's. Heal him. Don't let him die.

"Macken—"

"Okay, okay." She smiled for him. "I don't really know what to talk about."

"You'll think...of something."

She laughed. "Hey! That's charming. Well, I'm about to talk your ear off, so you'd better get ready, buster. Let's see..." She bit her lip. She had never told anyone else what she was about to tell him. "Well...sometimes, I still play music."

"Know that."

"I also write songs. I've been writing them all down in this notebook...that was in my office. I guess it's destroyed now, but I have a lot of them. Songs, that is. I don't know... I mean, I used to only sing songs other people had written for me. That's just how it works when you're a 'star.' I hate that word. Anyway, writing down my thoughts helps me process what's going on. Especially back when I didn't have anyone to talk to."

She clenched and unclenched her fingers. "It just seemed so natural to put them to music. What I was feeling, what I wanted to say to God. Things I was learning."

"Sing." His voice was a whisper.

Mackenzie didn't think about it.

"The air is still, silence all around.
But You are there.
My heart cries, 'Lord come and save me.'
You are there.
The final curtain falls, flowers fade and clouds come
in.
You are the light that breaks the night, bringing
morning.
The Son that gives His life, bringing freedom.
Jesus, You are there."

She kept singing, wondering why she had spent so many
years trying so hard to please a God who simply loved her
without demands. Sabine was right that she'd been too
stubborn to listen.

Well, no more.

Mackenzie had nothing to atone for. God had forgiven
her—she just hadn't found the courage to accept it enough
to forgive herself. But she would, because she could be
free of that burning, gnawing need to make up for the
girl she'd been.

Thank You, Lord.

She looked down at Aaron and the sound died on her
lips.

"Aaron?" Mackenzie touched his shoulder and shook
him gently. "Aaron, are you awake?"

Eyes closed, his lips parted to expel a breath.

"Aaron, don't do this. You have to wake up."

Aaron couldn't move. His whole body was numb. Why
was that? And why was he floating? From what sounded

like the end of a tunnel someone was singing. The voice was full and rich and very familiar.

She sang of light and morning.

Of life.

If he could wake up, he would tell her that he loved her. See the smile on her face when he did, knowing it would surprise her.

For as long as he could remember, he'd been living a shadow of a life. Going through the motions but keeping his heart guarded so closely that he didn't feel anything. Not even his brother ever truly got through.

What he needed was...Mackenzie. That was who was singing. Her sweet voice warmed him where there had been only cold and pain. Love rushed through his cells and awakened every part of him to the fact that he was completely hers.

If he could only wake up, then everything would be all right.

God, I want to be with her. Was it was even possible? *You brought me this woman to love. So I know You can get us out of here.*

So that he could love her, because that was what he was born to do. Mackenzie was made for him and him for her. He'd never believed in that stuff before, but he wanted to accept it. There was nothing else he could do except trust God.

In his personal life, or his professional life, it was the same—he simply needed to trust God for all things.

Aaron felt as though he was being lifted. Pain tore through his body, and he groaned.

"Aaron?"

He blinked. The rotors of a helicopter beat above his head. Wheels scraped concrete, and he blinked again.

Mackenzie's face was right there. He tried to smile but everything hurt too much.

She touched his face, her skin so soft. He closed his eyes.

"Stay with me."

He needed to tell her. Aaron tried to summon all the strength he had, but it was hard. "Love you."

"Stay with me, Aaron."

His lips formed the words. "Love you."

And then there was nothing.

Mackenzie's foot tapped a staccato beat on the tile floor. National news played at a low volume on a small TV tucked in the corner of the ceiling in the hospital waiting room. People passed by the door, going about their business. Nurses, doctors. Across the room an elderly couple sat in silence, holding hands. The hum of noise was like a swarm of bees, relentless and threatening to drive her insane.

Mackenzie squeezed her fingers together, wrung her hands until the joints in her fingers ached. After firefighters had made a way through the rubble of the center, they had found her and a barely breathing Aaron just in time. Movement had erupted, people suddenly rushing and shouting instructions, and she was escorted to an ambulance so they could check her out. But what was the point if he wasn't okay?

Aaron had been freed from under the water heater, and the decision had been made to airlift him to the closest hospital because there was no time to lose.

Barely hanging on.

Those words would stay with her for the rest of her life.

Mackenzie went with him, which meant she got to see that one glorious moment when he'd opened his eyes. The words he had mouthed set her heart to flight, but then his heart had stopped beating and the paramedics had to shock him back to life. It was the most gut-wrenching thing she'd ever witnessed in her life.

Movement at the door caught her attention, but it wasn't the doctor. Sabine led Doug into the room. His hands were bandaged from digging at the rubble in an attempt to burrow down to the last place he'd seen them.

Mackenzie stood. Her legs were stiff from sitting for so long, and they gave out. Sabine yelped and Doug lunged for her. Mackenzie managed to grab his forearms, avoiding his injuries, but he still winced. "Sorry."

Doug helped her sit. "Don't apologize. You've been through enough tonight."

"Yes." Sabine settled on his other side, looking around him at Mackenzie. "How are you doing?"

"Bruises on my knees and some scratches, but nothing more than feeling as if I got pummeled. Not like—"

Doug lifted his elbow, and she grasped it like a lifeline. He gave her a small smile. "Have the doctors told you anything?"

"I'm not a relative, and I've asked for an update so many times they've started ignoring me. As far as I know, he's still in surgery."

Eric tore through the door. "Mackenzie, thank God you're okay."

He swept Mackenzie up in a hug. She held on even tighter, reveling in the feel of strong arms around her. A sob worked its way up in her throat.

"I thought you were in jail."

"My office got a package. Proof that my partner was the mole responsible for every file that was leaked. He was colluding with Eva, so he was the link between her and the Carosas, too. I still had a lot to explain to them before they would believe me, but when Doug called and told them what happened to Aaron, they let me come."

"So you're not free?"

"I'll be fine. It's mostly just paperwork from this point." His eyes strayed over her shoulder to where Doug was, and something passed across his features that she couldn't discern.

"But—"

Eric gave her one last squeeze and then released her. "I've already seen the doctor. I figured it couldn't hurt to have a federal badge in their faces to make them cough up some information, so I went straight there. They're sending someone in right away."

Mackenzie sucked in a breath and nodded. "Thank you, Eric."

He squeezed her hand.

True to his words, a white haired man in blue scrubs strode in. "I'm Dr. Palmer."

He shook Eric's hand. "I understand it was a water heater that fell on him?"

Mackenzie nodded. The doctor turned back to Eric. "The weight crushed his left patella, and he has multiple fibula and tibia fractures. He'll need further surgeries to repair the damage since we had to stabilize him first. The injury to his torso was more extensive—"

Eric gasped. "More?"

Mackenzie's breath evaporated.

"I'm afraid the shard of wood was long. It entered his right side just below his ribs and cut through his diaphragm, puncturing his lung. We repaired that damage, but all in all you're talking about months of downtime in order to heal. Aaron has a long road ahead of him, but I'm confident he will recover."

"But not fully." Doug's words were somber.

The doctor gave them a small conciliatory smile. "We won't know for some time. Right now, Aaron is stable. The nurse will let you know when he's ready for visits, as long as you keep it short."

Mackenzie stepped away from the huddle. She'd been so happy just knowing he was alive. What if he didn't recover all of his mobility? She squeezed her eyes shut. He might never be able to be a solider again.

God, give him comfort. Give us the words to say. Help him through this.

She stumbled back and sank hard into a chair.

An hour later she walked into a dimly lit hospital room. Monitors beeped a steady rhythm to mark each heartbeat, each breath. Eric turned away, but she'd seen the sheen of tears in his eyes. He crossed to Mackenzie and squeezed her forearm as they passed each other in the doorway.

Aaron's face was too pale, his fingers too cold. She held his hand between both of hers, trying to give him some of her heat, and leaned down and put her lips to his forehead. The last words he spoke to her played in her head.

"I love you, too."

TWENTY-THREE

Aaron eyed the small cream-colored plastic pitcher. Condensation beaded on the outside, making his mouth dry just looking at it. He swallowed, tasting fuzz and an odd chemical. His chest was wrapped with layer upon layer of bandages. It was as if he had a flak jacket on. The pain was dull but present enough that he wasn't going to try to move anytime soon.

If only the water was closer.

He stretched out his hand for the pitcher but couldn't get near enough to grab it on the high table beside his hospital bed. He grunted, testing the limit of his reach without moving the rest of his body.

Useless. Just like he was now. Just like he'd caused Franklin to be.

If he twisted, bent or leaned the wrong way, he knew his chest would be on fire. He wasn't even going to think about his legs, except for flexing his toes every so often just to make sure there was some sense of functionality.

They were still there, and he could feel them, which meant things could have gone a lot worse. He'd seen army brothers who were amputees and had more than a ton of respect for how they dealt with it. Mostly, Aaron was just thankful to be alive. He wasn't going to think about what could have happened if the water heater had landed anywhere other than on one of his legs.

The damage to his torso from the wood was enough that even an inch difference and he wouldn't be lying here. How could he be anything other than overwhelmed with thanks to God for still having, at least, his life? After so many years of taking it for granted, it seemed strange to be grateful just to be able to breathe in and out. Life itself was a gift. Why hadn't he noticed that before?

But he *was* thirsty.

He reached again for the pitcher. The door to his matchbox-size room opened and he nearly groaned. He wasn't too happy about having to undergo another round of poking and prodding by perky nurses who were seriously annoying, or doctors who looked down their noses and nodded a lot. He'd rather they all left him alone with his prognosis. He would let them know if he needed anything.

No one else could help him process the idea that he couldn't be a solider anymore. Why did they think a counselor would help him? He just needed time. And space.

Whoever had come in was close to the side of the bed.

"Want some help?"

Mackenzie's voice brought with it a rush of vitality that made him feel as though he could leap from the bed. Visions of pulling her into his arms, dipping and kissing her brought a smile to his face. But he kept his eyes focused on the prize, still reaching to the opposite side for the water. She didn't need to know how desperately he didn't want her to leave. But she would. Eventually she'd have to decide where she was going to go now that the threat was over.

"Aaron? Do you need a drink?"

Why was she still here? Did she really think she was helping him when it was torture having to smell her vanilla perfume and pretend he didn't see how upset she was? It was as though she was taking the end of his career worse than he was.

He sighed. If only it was an inch closer or if he could roll the table nearer... He gripped the edge and pulled. Mackenzie reached across him to help, but not fast enough.

The table jerked and the pitcher toppled and fell over, dousing the whole surface with ice water. It ran onto the bed, bathing his hip in water. He groaned at the pain.

Mackenzie rushed around the bed. She pulled the table away and ducked into the bathroom, came out with a towel and began mopping up the mess—including his side.

He bit back what he really wanted to say. If she wanted to baby him, fine. But he didn't have to like it.

"I'll get you some more water, okay?"

He didn't answer.

Mackenzie stilled beside him. In the corner of his vision, her white knuckles gripped the towel in her hands. He looked up. Her eyes were soft, but she was trying to hold it back. As though she didn't want him to know she pitied him.

"Will you let me help you?"

Honestly, Aaron wasn't sure he even knew how to do that. Yeah, he was alive. But he hated feeling so helpless, wondering why this had to happen. God could have brought him out of that basement with no injuries, yet here he was: incapacitated, his career almost over. His future for once not clear, but shrouded so that he couldn't see what lay ahead.

Where would he be in a year? What would become of him? He hoped Mackenzie would still be here, but he didn't want her to see him so weak. Couldn't she come back when he was strong again?

Mackenzie sighed. "Here, take this." She pulled a bottle of water from her purse and twisted the lid off before handing it to him.

Aaron gritted his teeth. He could have opened it himself. Maybe. Okay, probably not, but he didn't need her making it so obvious. Next thing she'd be trying to cut his meat for him...when they let him have some.

He watched her walk out the door and sighed. Why couldn't he be a better man? One who knew how to say what he was thinking and feeling. He stared at the closed door and listened to the click of seconds on the wall clock.

The handle turned, and Aaron fought the urge to roll his eyes. Wouldn't anyone let him have five minutes of peace?

Eric stuck his head in and a smile immediately broke over his face. "Brother, you look like death warmed over."

"Thanks." He sounded like a frog. Aaron cleared his throat before he took another sip of Mackenzie's room-temperature water. It would do until she got back with the pitcher. Eric sat in the chair beside the bed, the one Mackenzie had slept in, insisting she needed to be with him even when the nurses had told her she should go home. He was sure it wasn't comfortable at all, but she hadn't complained. "They pulled Carosa's body out of the rubble this morning. Single shot to the forehead. You don't mess around, do you?"

"It wasn't me."

"Then, who—"

"Eva. Did they find her body, too?"

Eric set one foot on his opposite knee. "Under a pile of concrete. It wasn't pretty, but she's gone now. She can't hurt Mackenzie anymore."

"What about your job?"

"I'm headed to a meeting with my boss next. The charges were dropped since Doug managed to find enough proof Schweitzer was the mole, but that reporter still outed me as a WITSEC inspector. I need to find out if I'm being fired, or transferred to another part of the marshals."

Aaron nodded.

Mackenzie swept back in. "Eric, it's so good to see you."

Eric rose and enveloped her in a hug. "You, too, Mackenzie. You look lovely."

She tucked hair behind her ear with slender fingers. "If you say so."

Aaron sniffed. "Did you bring my water?"

She turned to him then, the warmth in her eyes deepening. "Yes, with ice." She took the bottle and handed him a cup with a straw. He tossed the straw onto the table and took big gulps, downing the entire cup before lifting it up for her.

"I guess you were thirsty."

Eric coughed, sounding a lot like he was laughing. "Well, I just thought I'd check in, but since you're in such good hands I'm going to leave you two to it."

"I actually need to talk to you a minute." Mackenzie motioned to the door. "Can we step outside?"

Aaron pressed his lips together. What was all this about? Why did she need to speak privately with his brother?

Eric reached out to shake Aaron's hand. "Take care."

Aaron held on a second longer and gave it an extra squeeze. "Sure. You, too."

Mackenzie closed the door behind them and pulled the piece of paper from her back pocket. "I signed it."

Eric grinned. "Does it feel good knowing the threat is over, that you don't need to be in WITSEC anymore?"

She blew out a breath, trying to push off the stress of being around Aaron when he was this closed off. And of not knowing what the future was going to bring for them, pleased. "There was nothing good about what happened. Now I just want to forget it and try to salvage what's left of my career."

Sabine sat back in her seat. "I'm sorry. I shouldn't have said anything."

Aaron blew out a breath and pulled into a supermarket parking lot. "Where are you going to go now?"

Sabine was silent for a minute and then sighed. "Don't worry about me. Like Doug said, we'll help Eric any way we can until this clears."

Aaron nodded.

Then Sabine said, "And don't worry about the colonel, either. He knows what happened wasn't your fault. Franklin is alive, and the guys will come around."

Aaron's jaw flexed as though he was grinding his teeth. Mackenzie watched the byplay between them. She'd had hints before now that something had happened to Aaron. This wasn't just about his shoulder injury; it seemed as though something more had gone on. And Sabine knew what it was.

If she pressed him, would he open up to her? He'd inferred she didn't need to know all the details of his life to trust him, but she couldn't help wanting to see if she might be able to make it better. Only that would make Aaron a project, just like all the kids in the center. Did she want that to define their friendship?

Being his counselor was not a good idea. She might forever define their relationship as something she didn't want it to be. She might have a degree, but she wasn't a licensed therapist.

Something had to change for him. He seemed so torn up about whatever it was that he lashed out when anyone tried to tend the wound that was inside him. And now he was channeling the anger, the pain of…whatever it was, only what her heart was telling her. But she could hardly throw herself at him in his condition.

"Are you okay?"

Mackenzie huffed out a laugh. "I honestly have no idea. Things are all so up in the air right now I'm not sure what to do, or if I should even just go. Aaron doesn't seem to want me here."

Eric squeezed her shoulder. "God hasn't brought you this far to let go of you now. And as much as Aaron might act like he doesn't want you around, he would be even more insufferable if you left."

Mackenzie laughed. "Thank you. I needed to hear that." She smiled. "It's going to be strange not having you around in case I need something. But I feel lighter now that Carosa is gone. I'm just not used to it yet."

"You have the rest of your life to get used to that feeling, Mackenzie. And I'll always be just a phone call away, okay? No matter what happens with you and Aaron."

She nodded, and Eric pulled her in for a tight hug. "Take care."

"You, too."

Mackenzie had been back in the room half an hour, but still neither of them had said anything.

Aaron held her gaze, knowing there was a lot to say. But the energy he had was fading, making him wonder why she insisted on hanging here with him. "Don't feel like you have to stay." He settled back against the pillows. "I think I'm going to take a nap."

Mackenzie pulled a magazine from her purse and settled back in the chair. "I'm fine right here."

Aaron closed his eyes, but he could still see her. This woman was with him, in his mind, his heart. He could see her eyes, full of fear, and feel her hand touching his cheek. Why couldn't he just tell her what he wanted?

Stay with me.

But she was staying with him in his hospital room, without even asking him if that was what he needed. Not in a pushy way, more like quietly letting him know that she cared. What had he ever done to deserve this? Aaron exhaled, falling asleep with Mackenzie's name on his lips.

TWENTY-FOUR

The sound was so slight. Mackenzie looked up, certain she had heard him breathe her name. Like a sigh or a prayer. He seemed so distant, always holding back, as though he was forcing himself not to explode, which was what he really wanted to do. It was obvious he was frustrated by the situation. Anyone would be.

Recovering from surgery, talking with doctors about more procedures, unable to get up or do much of anything without help. He seemed as if he was trying to convince them all that everything was fine. Why couldn't he talk to her instead of holding it in all the time?

God, help us know what to say to each other. Give me the words that will touch his heart.

Mackenzie went to his side and perched on the edge of the bed. She watched the rise and fall of his chest, tucked her hand in his and spoke, keeping her voice low. "I want you to know something. I've felt it for a while and I'm thinking… Well, it just seems like the right time to tell you. I know you're uncertain about what's going to happen, unsure what the future holds for you, but I want you to know that you can do anything. I really believe that you'll find the path, because if anyone can, then it's you."

She stroked her thumb over the back of his hand.

"You're always so strong and together, as if you know who you are. Sure, I'd love it if you told me what you're feeling. Or how you're doing sometimes, just so I know where you're at. But that's okay. It's part of who you are. And, well...I love you."

Warmth enveloped her, and she could finally accept the fact that she didn't want to live her life without Aaron being part of it. But how would it ever work? What would they do?

She bit her lip and blinked back tears. "I don't know what's going to happen. I don't really know where to go now or what I'm supposed to do. I guess we're in the same boat that way. And maybe that doesn't have to be a scary thing, because we can navigate it together. We could find a way to make this work, to stay together."

She blew out a breath that shuddered in her chest. A lump had worked its way up to lodge in her throat.

"I wish we could do that. I've gotten used to you being around all the time. If you left, or you told me to go—" Her voice broke. "I don't know what I'd do."

The bed shifted, and a motor whirred as the head of the bed rose. Mackenzie looked up. Aaron's eyes were down, focused on his finger pressing the button. What was he doing? When he was finally upright, he looked up at her.

She blinked and tears ran down her face. Mackenzie opened her mouth, but he covered it with his fingers, cutting off the sound.

"I love you, too."

She stared at him. "I thought you were asleep."

He sighed. "I should have told you. I'm not so good at all this emotions stuff. You're going to have to stick with me as I navigate it. Maybe we could row that boat together, too?"

His lips curled up at the corners. He was teasing her.

She sat up straight, folding her arms and trying to act as though she was mad. "Are you making fun of me? Because I was pouring out my heart, and I don't think it was very funny at all."

He touched her cheek, the roughness of his palm abrading her skin. Mackenzie closed her eyes as his fingers slid into her hair. The facade of being mad evaporated, and warmth hummed through her.

"I said I loved you."

She didn't open her eyes, but she did purse her lips. "I heard you."

"And all that stuff you said? I'm in. So long as you add a small wedding at this private beach I heard about. But I'm only dancing one song. And we're going on a honeymoon. As for the rest of it, we'll have to see how things play out. I have some ideas, but one thing I do know is that wherever you are, that's where I'm gonna be."

His words echoed in her mind and she held her breath.

Aaron laughed. "You might wanna breathe, babe."

"Yes."

He tipped his head back, smiling full on now. Mackenzie smiled back, and he tugged her toward him.

"I don't want to hurt you more."

For the first time, his eyes were open all the way to his soul and Mackenzie saw the answers to everything she wanted to know, right there on his face. He continued to pull her close, so Mackenzie put her hands to the bed on either side of him, keeping her weight from pressing on his injury.

Aaron motioned to her with his chin. "Come here, Mackenzie. I wanna kiss you."

When she leaned in to kiss him, she was smiling. Aaron's hand went to the back of her head, holding her close as their lips moved in a melody that soared. She shifted and touched his cheek with one hand, feeling the warmth of his skin. So alive.

She pulled back and touched her forehead to his, seeing the smile playing on his lips.

You brought him back to me. Thank You, Lord.

Mackenzie found there, in that moment, that she didn't need a cause. She didn't need anyone to save. She could live her life content, because she would be with him. There would be no protection team, or marshals there to help her navigate her life now, but she certainly wouldn't be alone.

She would never be alone again.

EPILOGUE

Mackenzie waited at the edge of the crowd of people milling on a downtown Dallas street. Thankfully it wasn't yet nine o'clock in the morning, so instead of being deathly hot, the heat was only mildly oppressive.

Aaron walked toward her, a smile playing on his lips. He wore the khaki pants and light blue button-down shirt with ease, as though looking that good was the most natural thing in the world. It still astounded her, every time she looked at him, that a guy like him could fall for a girl so far from the put-together star she'd been.

The limp in his stride from his injury was still there. He'd thrown away the cane weeks before everyone thought he should have and declared that he refused to be an invalid any longer. Mackenzie had warred between being concerned he'd reinjure himself and being intensely proud of him for the fight he showed in working toward recovery. Together they'd found new direction, a shared dream for the future.

She brushed her hand down the skirt of her blue dress, a shade darker than his shirt. He must have seen her bite her lip, because when he drew close to her, his arms slid around her waist. His kiss was light but lingered. "You don't have anything to worry about. You look beautiful."

He kissed her again.

Mackenzie chuckled. "We have to go. We're late already and everyone's waiting for us."

He gave a mock sigh. "I suppose. Ready?"

Aaron squeezed her hand, and they picked their way through the crowd to the front doors. They had bought this former theater for a song and spent months—and a considerable chunk of change—to establish this place. This was the legacy of what their lives would be about, no longer atonement.

Mackenzie stopped at the front of the crowd, where people had created a pocket of space just outside the front doors of the Lani Anders Center for the Arts and Sports Complex.

The mayor's assistant saw Mackenzie and motioned for her to come to the front. She walked to the perky young woman, smiling as if she wasn't nervous at all, and faced the crowd. It had been a long time since she was the center of attention. She squinted in the sun's glare, and Aaron gave her a thumbs-up.

Mackenzie stood beside the mayor, shaking hands. She held the pose while photographers snapped a million pictures of her smile frozen in place. When he finally let go of her hand, he gave her a hilariously large pair of scissors. She turned to the wide red ribbon pinned across the front doors of her new dream.

She hesitated and glanced at Aaron, but he smiled to encourage her to go ahead. She held out her hand to him, and her fiancé didn't hesitate before coming to her side. His hand rubbed between her shoulder blades and cameras erupted in flashes.

Together they snipped the ribbon, officially opening the new center. It was a twin of the one her staff in Phoenix now ran. After the old center had blown up, a number of local benefactors had emerged, willing to rebuild the place despite everything that had happened there. Mackenzie had been overjoyed that they believed in her vision of bringing the arts to inner-city kids, and immediately commenced talks to open a new center. But Arizona wasn't where she was supposed to be.

The kids at the center in Phoenix were all at different stages of their recovery. They would be fine, but they didn't need Mackenzie when there were good people still there.

When Aaron had suggested Dallas, she'd been cautious about moving. Then the moment she stepped off the plane, she knew it was the place for her...for them.

The noise of the crowd soared with cheers. Aaron leaned down and touched her lips with his.

With the business of the ceremony done, people poured inside to tour the new facility and the sports complex that was attached to it. Sabine had been jealous that the view from Mackenzie's window would be a bunch of guys showing off their talents. Mackenzie had laughed with her friend. Now she would see Aaron at the sports complex every day from where she worked in the performing-arts portion of this new center and know he was always close to her.

The top floor of the building was being renovated into a condo. Right now Mackenzie was living with Aaron's pastor friend—another old army buddy of his—and the guy's wife. Aaron was sleeping on a mat on the floor of what would be their home after they were married. Despite her concern, he'd insisted on doing the bulk of the renovations himself, and she had to admit he was doing a fantastic job.

She fingered the simple diamond on her left hand. In a month she would be walking down the aisle to him. She couldn't wait.

A TV anchorwoman toddled over to Mackenzie on her four-inch spike heels. A big guy carrying a camera on his shoulder followed close behind. The woman cracked a perfect smile and stuck her microphone in Mackenzie's face. "Lani, darling! Tell the viewers what it was like being on the run in witness protection."

Mackenzie smiled. "It's been a long time, Adelyn, but I wouldn't trade the journey for anything else. Sometimes life throws you a curveball and you have to move with it, or let it pass you by." She glanced at Aaron, talking to the mayor. "I'm glad I didn't let opportunity slip through my fingers."

"Delightful! And who is this?"

Mackenzie turned as Aaron slid an arm around her waist. "This is my fiancé. Aaron is a former soldier and the brains behind the sports-complex side of the center. All of the staff are former servicemen and women who have made tremendous sacrifices for this country. It is our great honor to have them come alongside to help serve the young people of this community, young people so often dismissed or overlooked."

Mackenzie didn't think it was possible to smile any wider, but she did. "I can tell you, I am one extremely blessed woman."

"Sounds like it. How wonderful!" A sly smile lifted the anchorwoman's mouth. "And when is the wedding?"

Mackenzie could have laughed out loud. Reporters were always trying to get details of the small ceremony they were planning. Aaron squeezed her hand and answered for her. "Less than four weeks and I get to make this incredible woman my wife. Can you imagine? Talk about being extremely blessed."

The anchorwoman wrinkled her nose, probably upset that she wasn't going to get anything juicy out of them.

"Thank you for talking with us today, and best wishes for your venture."

The anchorwoman moved away and Mackenzie turned to Aaron.

He kissed her. The noise of the crowd dimmed as he swept her up in the moment and the sweetness of his strength. After a minute, he leaned back. "I came over here to tell you something. I forget what it is, though."

She laughed.

"Right, now I remember." He glanced back over his shoulder. "There's someone here to see you."

Mackenzie looked past him, to a face she hadn't seen in years. The sight of her mother, thinner and so much older than she remembered, brought tears to her eyes. It had taken weeks after Aaron's accident and the drama with Carosa being over before she found the courage to look up her mom and dad.

Mackenzie's father had passed away a number of years before from liver cancer. Her mom had been living alone in a condo in Miami. At first their communication had been awkward, neither really knowing what to say to each other. But when Mackenzie began to open up about what the years had been like and what she had come to realize about God's grace, her mom had broken down, crying over the phone. It turned out that her mom had discovered a relationship with God after Mackenzie's dad died and she'd been praying for her daughter every day since.

The relief, the joy that they could have a relationship where they had both moved on from the past, was indescribable. It wouldn't be an easy road, but both of them wanted to begin anew. Like so many things in their lives had.

Aaron squeezed her shoulder and whispered in her ear, "Go say hi to her."

Mackenzie shot him a smile and crossed the distance to where her mom stood off to the side of the building's entrance. She stopped short a ways away, suddenly unsure of herself despite all she'd accomplished. Mackenzie looked at the sidewalk, praying no one noticed her discomfort. This was the woman who let her walk away, valuing her own lifestyle more than her daughter. She took a deep breath and looked up, finding a smile she didn't have to force.

But when she looked at Clara Anders now, Mackenzie saw nothing of the woman from years ago. Instead there was only delight in the eyes full of tears.

Mackenzie stepped closer. "Hi, Mom."

"Mackenzie." Clara expelled a lungful of air. "That sounds so strange, calling you that. Are you really going to keep that name?"

Mackenzie nodded. "It's who I am now."

Her mom nodded. "I wasn't sure before, but looking at you now, I understand."

She wrapped her arms around her mom. It took a second, but the smaller woman reached up and did the same. Tears ran down her face.

"This is a wonderful thing you and Aaron are doing here. You should be very proud of yourself." When they broke apart, Clara smiled. "I met your young man."

Mackenzie had a rush of nerves wondering what her mom thought of him.

"He's wonderful. I'm very happy you found the man God made just for you." Clara's eyes dimmed. "Your father was that man for me."

Mackenzie stiffened, not really wanting to dredge up what was gone.

Her mom continued, "Somewhere along the way, we lost our direction. But from the beginning there wasn't a doubt we were it for each other. There's never been anyone else for me, then or since." Clara shook her head. "Don't mind me. I'm happy for you, my darling."

"Thanks, Mom. That means a lot to me."

"And can I hope that I'll be part of your life going on?" A wistful smile crossed her face. "I quite like the thought of being a grandmother."

Mackenzie laughed. "I'd like that, too. But we'll have to see what time brings."

She might have missed a lot of years and have a lot of history with her mom that both of them would rather forget, but that didn't mean the future couldn't be bright. She loved the idea of her mom being a part of their lives and the lives of the kids she and Aaron might have together. They could leave the bad stuff in the past and forge a new family dynamic together. Build for their children what she and Aaron never had.

Thinking of him…she turned and scanned the faces around them. He was talking with Pastor John.

As though he felt her gaze on him, he looked up and caught her staring. His face brightened into a smile, and she wondered that this man who had been so contrary and who held everything so close to himself, never giving away his feelings, now practically glowed with joy.

He crossed the room, stepping around people milling and talking, partaking of refreshments. He ignored a waiter's offer of a flute of sparkling grape juice and made a beeline for her.

He slipped his arms around her waist. "Caught you."

"You certainly did. And I'm glad. Very glad." The rush of emotion brought tears to her eyes.

"Hey, no crying. This is a happy day, remember. What's going on?"

She sniffed. "No crying. I'll try to remember that."

He gave her a gentle shake. "What's up?"

"I'm just really glad you found me and I found you, and God brought us together. Or however that all works. I'm just glad it did."

He cleared his throat. "Me, too. You have no idea how alone I felt before you came along. And you wouldn't let me do what I'd always done. Thank God you weren't content to let me hold back. You'd have walked away and I would have been…well, it definitely wouldn't have been pretty. At all."

One corner of his mouth tipped up. "I'd probably be sitting in my boat, all alone with two days' worth of stubble and a fishing pole that I'd run out of bait for, wondering where on earth I'd gone wrong."

Mackenzie laughed. "I love you."

"And I love you."

* * * * *

Dear Reader,

Thank you so much for reading this book, my second story with Love Inspired Suspense.

The twists and turns of life often lead us to places we never expected. But it's through these detours that God brings us to the place where He wants us to be. Only then can we fully experience the fullness of His love and faithfulness toward us.

That's what I've learned. It doesn't matter where your feet take you, God will always bring you to the place where your heart can hear what He wants to say.

To find out more about me and my books, you can go to www.authorlisaphillips.com or you can email me at lisaphillipsbks@gmail.com. If you're not online, you can write to me c/o Love Inspired Books, 233 Broadway, Suite 1001, New York, NY 10279.

I would love to hear from you.

God bless you richly,

Lisa Phillips

Questions for Discussion

1. At the beginning of the story, Mackenzie was alone and a target. What do you think gave her the strength to not crack under that pressure?

2. Have you ever been in a situation where you were targeted for one reason or another? How did it work out?

3. Aaron was recovering from a mission where, his first time up to bat as team leader, everything went wrong. Have you ever had a circumstance in your life where everything went wrong?

4. Aaron believed his failure meant everyone he worked with, everyone he loved, will reject him. Have you ever felt that way? If you've learned otherwise, what made you change your mind?

5. Eric was essentially Aaron's entire family. What do you think caused them to be estranged, given the deep bond between them?

6. What do you think of Aaron's desire to reconnect with his brother and the timing of it, coming on the heels of his failed mission?

7. Have you ever tried to reconnect with someone with whom you're estranged? What were the results?

8. When Aaron and Mackenzie made the decision to investigate Eric's coworkers in order to find the mole,

what did you think of their decision, given that it posed a risk to their safety?

9. Doug and Sabine, whose story was told in *Double Agent,* were Aaron's closest friends. Do you have people in your life who will drop everything to help you out?

10. After receiving the package, Aaron started to believe things might work out after all. Have you ever experienced someone reaching out to you that gave you hope in a dark time?

11. Eva's betrayal of Mackenzie came as a surprise to her. Have you had someone in your life who did this to you? How did you overcome it?

12. Mackenzie's guilt over the life she lived as a pop star stayed with her for years. Do you have things in your past you regret? If you've moved past these things, how have you done it?

13. Mackenzie sacrificed herself to save Aaron and his friends. What did you think of her decision?

14. Aaron raced to rescue Mackenzie from Carosa, but when the bombs went off, they don't make it out of the building. In that moment, God was their comfort. Can you think of a time in your life God has done that for you?

15. Aaron and Mackenzie began their own center, together, with bright hope for the future. Why do you think they chose to do this in particular?

COMING NEXT MONTH FROM
Love Inspired® Suspense

Available October 7, 2014

THE LAWMAN RETURNS
Wrangler's Corner • by Lynette Eason
When his brother is murdered, deputy Clay Starke is
determined to find the killer. Could beautiful social worker
Sabrina Mayfield hold the missing clue?

DOWN TO THE WIRE
SWAT: Top Cops • by Laura Scott
Someone has planted a bomb under schoolteacher Tess Collins's
desk and only explosives expert Declan Shaw can save her.
Together they must figure out how she became the obsession of
a madman before she becomes the next victim.

HOLIDAY DEFENDERS
by Debby Giusti, Susan Sleeman and Jodie Bailey
When danger strikes at Christmastime, these military heroes are
ready to give their all for their country—and for the women they
love.

COVERT CHRISTMAS
Echo Mountain • by Hope White
Search and Rescue K-9 dog handler Breanna McBride witnesses
Scott Becket getting shot and comes to his aid. Realizing he has
amnesia, Breanna and Scott try and retrace his steps to remember
his past, but soon discover some things are better left forgotten....

TUNDRA THREAT • by Sarah Varland
When McKenna Clark stumbles across a double homicide in
the Alaskan tundra, the wildlife trooper knows she's in over her
head. But that doesn't mean she'll let former crush
Will Harrison help with the investigation—until they find that
she's become the attacker's new target.

KEEPING WATCH • by Jane M. Choate
Someone is stalking Danielle Barclay, and her bodyguard,
former Delta Force soldier Jake Rabb, will stop at nothing to
keep her safe. Even if it means putting his own life in danger.

**LOOK FOR THESE AND OTHER LOVE INSPIRED BOOKS WHEREVER
BOOKS ARE SOLD, INCLUDING MOST BOOKSTORES, SUPERMARKETS,
DISCOUNT STORES AND DRUGSTORES.**